Wakefield Press

DARK DREAMS

Heather Millar is a freelance writer and editor who has worked on a range of magazines and books in Australia and England.

Sonja Dechian is a writer and researcher with ABC TV in Adelaide. She has a Masters in Creative Writing as well as a graduate diploma in science communication. She has been published in a range of magazines and journals. Sonja's unpublished manuscript was highly commended in the 2002 Adelaide Festival Awards for literature.

Eva Sallis is a writer best known for her literary fiction. Her novels include *Hiam*, *The City of Sealions* and *Mahjar*. She has co-edited a number of anthologies. She is current President of Australians Against Racism.

DARK DREAMS

AUSTRALIAN REFUGEE STORIES
by young writers aged 11–20 years

Edited by Sonja Dechian, Heather Millar
and Eva Sallis

Wakefield
Press

Wakefield Press
16 Rose Street
Mile End
South Australia 5031
wakefieldpress.com.au

First published 2004
Reprinted 2004, 2005, 2011, 2013, 2014, 2017

Cover illustration by Fontaine Anderson (originally created for
West Domestic Violence Centre)
Cover designed by Liz Nicholson, designBITE
Text designed and typeset by Clinton Ellicott

National Library of Australia Cataloguing-in-publication entry

Dark dreams: Australian refugee stories.
ISBN 978 1 86254 629 5.

1. Short stories, Australian. 2. Refugees – Australia.
3. Refugees – Social aspects – Australia. I. Millar, Heather, 1963–   .
II. Sallis, Eva. III. Dechian, Sonja.

A820.8

CORIOLE
McLAREN VALE

CONTENTS

Foreword

by Eva Sallis

Dark Dreams: Australian Refugee Stories is both an extraordinary record of young people's literary talent and a collection of important and controversial Australian stories that need to be heard and read now. It also represents a far-reaching, quirky and unique view of Australia's social history. It is a collection of stories in which young writers remind their elders what Australia has been to displaced people in the past, and remind us graphically what it means, in many different variations, to be a refugee. It is a bleak collection, yes, but rich in idealism, energy and optimism. Throughout this book there is the recurrent theme of friendship – friendships lost, broken, remembered and found, now in Australia.

The stories in this book were collected in 2002 through an unprecedented nationwide schools competition, Australia IS Refugees!. The young writers were asked to find someone who came to Australia as a refugee and listen to their story. Then they had to imagine it and in a sense make it their own by writing it. Many children had one of these stories living in the memory of a relative and many found strangers who, through storytelling, became friends. Many others told their own or their parents' stories.

Here there are wry and quirky observations, skilled and well-researched essays, passionate defenses, moving and shocking stories, adventures, romances and successes; and stories of death and failure. Many works are also fine pieces of journalism. Many are highly creative, imaginative reinventions of a tale a writer has heard, focusing on what struck the author most. Some, 'the real treasures,' as Helen Garner put it, are stories of the author's own experience – young writers narrating and analysing for us what they have lived through in the recent past, or what happened in their immediate families not so long ago. Many others have an author put him or herself in the place of the subject and write as if experiencing directly what was in fact someone else's experience. Twelve-year-old Khazmira Bashah's beautiful and empathetic exploration of Mai Nguyen's story is an example which won the junior category of the competition. Such a leap of the creative imagination makes individual people visible and imaginable. Such a leap is all it takes for us to have a right compassion, not compassion that lumps people together as victims, but one that sees each human life as unique and irreplaceable.

In some cases, the interview encounter was the first time the writer had met someone they identified as a refugee, and several comment that this encounter changed their views completely. Some writers interpreted the idea of an interview very broadly, and, with an important tale to tell, told the stories of long dead relatives, even ancestors. In other cases, teachers invited people to come and speak to the class and the whole class responded, each writer in his or her way. The different, even contradictory stories that came out of this are deeply charming, especially among the younger age group. Taha's Story, told in two differing versions by two twelve-year-olds, shows clearly this transforming process, in which the final story reflects the author as much as the subject.

Some stories are so grim and sad that the fresh voice of the narrator is the only brightness. Jack Lander's telling of the life of Sadie Wagner shocks all the more for the fact that this twelve-year-old writer is able to communicate that Sadie's life could never be fully repaired after such experiences as he narrates.

Hai-Van Nguyen, the senior category winner, flew to Geneva to the United Nations with Margaret Reynolds in April 2003 as the major part of her prize. Her stunning, sad and inspiring essay closes this book. Her story about her parents' experiences is likely to become a classic of contemporary essay writing.

Most stories suggest an Australia to be proud of. But not all. Australia has also been a place of injustice and cruelty. Tshala Jenkins' story about blackbirding, the practice of enslaving Islanders to work on Australian plantations that brought her great grandparents here many generations ago, reminds us that Australia has not always been a safe or happy place, and is not just a land of migrants. Contemporary stories of refugees in detention often show young Australian writers' outrage along with the injustices of a system that imprisons men, women and children indefinitely and for no crime.

It is a measure of Australia in 2003 that these young voices are also contentious and controversial. We printed the winning stories in a commemorative booklet which we sent to MPs. Then Minister for the Department of Migration and Indigenous Affairs Phillip Ruddock MP wrote to me to congratulate Hai-Van Nguyen and to praise the project overall, but Melanie Poole's striking essay exploring the experiences in detention of Gyzele Osmani and her family provoked sixteen paragraphs in which he dismisses Melanie's essay and the experiences Gyzele Osmani lived through on the basis of the policies he has in place in detention centres. His words reveal the tragic fault-line in contemporary political thinking in Australia about refugees' experiences. Simply put, no 'procedures in place' defended from an office in Canberra can disprove or deny what an individual experiences first hand in a remote detention centre. Detainees are eye-witnesses of the failure of everything from basic medical services to 'culturally appropriate meals' to the 'closely monitored' conduct and performance of Australasian Correctional Management (ACM), the company that managed Australia's detention centres.

The stories may be diverse in the extreme but they share a striking unapologetic compassion and a natural sense of justice and the importance of human rights. These voices may provoke controversy, but that is because they are important and relevant.

These stories have been lightly edited, preserving the voice and rhythm of the author. We corrected spelling, punctuation or expression only where it interfered with sense. In some stories sections have been cut that contained background, or information more or less duplicated in other stories. Some have been tightened. Authors who use English as a second language offer something unique, a language put under pressure to express their ideas and experiences. This is preserved as much as possible. We have edited only where the errors are simply of spelling or the sense is obscured. These voices have vigour and spirit. The broken or unusual use of language releases a surprising energy.

Errors of fact are often left in place – most of these stories are young writers' reinventions of the world they encounter in their own experience or that of others. So if a young writer speaks of the white Australia policy in the 1860s, that is fine by us. There are many organic truths outside facts, and these stories are works of fiction, imagination and history all in one.

Australia IS Refugees! Competition began in February 2002 as no more than an ambitious idea. I drafted the project quickly, with a strong sense of its pull. Albert Shelling gave his generous permission to use his harrowing and uplifting story as an example, and Australia IS Refugees! was launched as the second major endeavour of Australians Against Racism. As soon as the project was launched, sponsors and teams of skilled volunteers joined me in implementing it. For sponsors and supporters, the project became a vehicle for expression of dissent and for attempting an inspiring and positive path forward. Sponsors for prizes and the high profile judges gave the project credibility and generated the enthusiasm with which it was taken up, because between them they told children that a refugee's story is an intrinsically valuable thing, and an experience to be proud of and to share. Professor Margaret Reynolds of United Nations Association Australia sponsored the major prize, a trip to Geneva for the UN sitting in 2003 for the winner of the high schools category; the Independent Education Union, Australian Education Union, Australian Education Union – South Australia, and the New South Wales Teachers Federation made substantial donations of prize moneys and promoted the project energetically; Allen & Unwin sponsored the senior second prize, with the National Committee for Human Rights Education. Private individuals also made extraordinary donations. Such a person, Selina, sponsored all the prize money of the junior category, $2600. Author Geraldine Brooks co-sponsored, with $1500, the money for First Prize in the senior category; also sponsored by John Kinsella and Raimond Gaita. Judges Tom Shapcott, Phillip Adams, Helen Garner, Libby Gleeson and Meme McDonald generously volunteered their time and expertise. Malcolm Fraser's early and ongoing endorsement of the project also gave it considerable momentum. Neil Monteith created and maintained the extraordinary website that is AAR's public face and a distribution point for stories and project news. Many other people put their time and money into the project, and in essential ways the project and this book could not have happened without them. The full list of sponsors is included in the acknowledgments.

These stories will remind you that these unbearable events did not happen far away, to people we pity from a distance – a view the nightly news, especially now, too easily encourages. These events and histories are carried in the heart and mind of the person next to you, these experiences are with us, beside us, in the hearts of our brothers and sisters. These stories give something important of Australia's collective living experience, along with the recognition that Australia can and should also bring healing, safety, equality, freedom and peace.

In the midst of what has become a human rights crisis for Australia, this book is refreshing, important, inspiring. These harrowing stories are no less harrowing for being told through the words and imaginative recreation of the young authors, but they are also somehow incarnated, made visible. These stories generate a special kind of belonging for their subjects that is illuminated by the delight and seriousness with which each author responded to his or her task.

Such creativity is profoundly transforming. This project gave its participants enough freedom to discover for themselves what it means to be a refugee or to value and express their own history as refugee. It is the hope of all involved that this will have a slow but direct impact on Australia's evolving community.

Eva Sallis, President of Australians Against Racism Inc, 2003

A DARK DREAM LEFT A MARK IN MY HEART

'I do feel a little better now that I have told everyone my story . . . Many of us have hidden secrets and pains from our journeys or sadness because of the loss of loved ones.'

What Does Australia Want?

by Lucy McBride, aged 18

I realise how ignorant I am – these boys speak of places I have never even heard of.

Sitting opposite me, they all look so 'normal' – like me or any other Australian teenager – yet I know that I cannot even begin to comprehend the atrocities they would have experienced during their short lives.

I ask them if they want to return to their home countries, and later realise, as I play back the tape, what a stupid question this is. They have fled violence, persecution and who knows what else. Why would anyone *want* to return? The decision is unanimous – they all want to stay.

I ask if it was hard to leave their respective countries, and as I listen to the question being posed, the naivety of it strikes me. I cringe. Of course it was hard. 'Hard' does not even begin to describe adequately what would perhaps be one of the most difficult things they will ever do.

For them it must seem as if Australia is a Utopia, and when I ask if there are any bad things about Australia, 'not really, not really,' comes one reply – to him Australia is a refuge, a dream because of its social, religious and political freedom. However, our nation does hold problems for these young people – social prejudices and isolation taint their existences here. They all miss their friends and family, agreeing that Australia's worst aspect is its lack of community, which is such a fundamental aspect of the cultures they have left behind. When they go outside, 'there is no one there.'

While contemplating these answers, I recall my arrival to the interview. Apprehensive at the prospect of interviewing these boys, students at a high school for people who have recently immigrated to Australia, my purpose was to gain an understanding of what it is like to be a refugee here. I arrived early, about ten minutes, just before lunchtime. I was shown to the room in which the interview would be conducted. The heater was turned on and I was told that there would be a number of boys arriving shortly, a fact I was surprised by, as I had thought I was interviewing girls. I considered my questions and concluded that they were very general and not gender based, so it would not matter. I considered the implications gender would have on our interaction, but the thought left my mind quickly. I'd figure it out. A teenage boy of African descent entered the room and we were left alone while others were collected from their respective classrooms. We sat down, eyeing each other apprehensively across the table. The heater coughed and spluttered loudly and we both laughed nervously, trying to ease the tension. The other boys entered, and the interview began.

I discover . . .

Civil war threw one boy's home country, Liberia, in western Africa, into turmoil. He said, 'People were fighting. Have war in the country.' Forced to leave when he was three years old, he has little or no recollection of this period in his life. To flee the violence he crossed the border to Guinea where he lived in a refugee camp. 'It was hard,' he said. This simple statement does little to describe the lifestyle he would have endured under such circumstances, and his response matches his understated, uncomplaining attitude. He remained in that camp for nine years. From there he flew to France, to Singapore, to Sydney and then finally arrived in Adelaide three months ago, accompanied only by an older brother. Now fifteen, he cannot recall a single good memory from this period, and when I tentatively inquired about his parents, he could only reveal to me that they had been killed. He does not know how.

Another young man originally lived in Yugoslavia. He and his family left a year ago. In Yugoslavia, he explained, although the war is over, the United Nations still maintains control and his parents made the 'choice' to leave. Despite surviving the danger and uncertainty of this civil conflict, they could no longer see a future for themselves in Yugoslavia, as the country's newfound state of 'peace' brought new problems of unemployment and few opportunities. The war itself was 'terrible'. After the conflict began, his family was continually moving, forced from place to place after each was bombarded and left in ruins. The exact date he began his nomadic existence is permanently etched in his mind. 'The first of May, 1991,' he recalls. He was only six years old. At seventeen he tells me of the pictures he sees in his head, of destroyed houses and dead bodies waiting to be identified. 'We were always in black,' he says and explains that the constant state of mourning was due to the deaths of countless neigh-bours, friends and relatives. He explains their attempts to forge a life amidst the destruction of their country, yet it is obvious their efforts were lost in a sea of violence, hatred and warfare. He tells of a house they lived in, 'the house was pretty . . . destroyed. My mother and my father, we tried to fix it up . . .' I ask myself: What would it be like to view such violence and destruction everyday? To have your mind filled with such images? It occurred to me that the influence of such atrocities as he had repeatedly experienced would cut so much deeper than I could possibly comprehend. It made me feel inadequate and horribly naive.

Despite the state Yugoslavia was in, it was still difficult for him to leave – to leave behind family and friends. 'They were always there . . . they were with me all the time . . .' Most remained in the country, but others also left, mainly settling in America or other parts of Australia. What strikes me as amazing is, despite all these experiences, or perhaps because of them, his manner is easygoing and his smile wide and friendly. His one wish is 'to make everyone happy!' When questioned about the possibility of peace in Yugoslavia, 'maybe, maybe,' came the unconvinced, yet optimistic, reply. As for his own future: he dreams of playing soccer like Beckham and finishing school. And, finally, to the world – 'Stop it. Stop fighting.'

My eyes now rest on a seventeen-year-old from Afghanistan. He sits quietly, anxiously waiting for me to begin my questions. After a few moments I realise that this boy is exactly what I, and the rest of Australia, have been reading about in the newspapers every day for over a year. He is an 'illegal' immigrant, seeking asylum in Australia. An image of this boy having to sit in front of customs officials flicks through my mind, and I suddenly do not want to ask him similar, intrusive questions about his life and his journey to Australia. He quickly tells me of his life in Afghanistan, after the Taliban took control. No one was allowed to practice their own religion or voice their own beliefs. The rules of the governing party were constantly changing and consequently people were forced to live in a state of uncertainty and fear of unjust persecution. When I asked whether he thought Afghanistan could ever exist in a state of peace, he shook his head. He did not even consider it a possibility.

One year ago, this boy's family spent most of their money paying for a passage to Australia, seeking a new life of opportunity and freedom. I am in awe of, and shocked by, the enormity of this sacrifice. These feelings are juxtaposed by the horrible irony of 'our' (the majority of Australians and the developed world) attitude towards life. We seem to take everything for granted yet others, such as this boy and his family, will give up everything to have a life that resembles ours. He travelled by boat from Pakistan to Australia, consequently ending up in Port

Hedland detention centre in Western Australia for three months. His overriding impression of detention is its immense boredom, and I wonder why the Government does not provide education or work for these people; something constructive to occupy the long hours, days and months spent in detention. I ask if he is conscious of what Australians think of him, and he hangs his head in shame. He looks at the table and will not lift his eyes to mine again. He promises to work hard and obey the law – and I am struck with an overwhelming sense of sympathy for him and the cruel irony of his situation – no one I know would have such ideals, such intentions and such noble ambitions. I also feel guilty – it is the Australian population, of which I am a part, who make him feel like this. Who are we to do so?

Although my aim for this interview was to learn about refugees, what I realised within the first few minutes did not directly concern them, but myself. I came to understand how severely tainted my own perspective of refugees was – despite never having known or met a refugee before. The influence of the media, however much one attempts to remain objective, is immense. It seeps into our subconscious, altering our views, creating prejudices and fear. The revelation of the 'normality' of these boys has come to prove this to me. Thus, although, these boys view Australia as a kind of 'Utopia', the attitudes of many Australians flaw this ideal. Australians must come to realise that our population – the very multicultural society on which Australians pride themselves – is mostly the result of a couple of hundred years of migration, people who bring with them parts of their own cultures, ideals and beliefs.

My overall impression of the boys was their dedication to achieve a better life. Their goals seem simple – to leave their current school and attend a mainstream high school, followed by university to study a range of fields: medicine, engineering and computer science. They each have so much to contribute to Australian society.

These students highlight issues facing so many people around the world. All had stories to tell, or to reluctantly allude to; they were chosen randomly and all their fellow students would have had similar, yet unique, experiences – war, struggle, aggression – a sad picture of our world. It left me wondering: what does this say for people all around the world? If these students are the lucky ones, as they consider themselves to be by living in Australia, how many people are in worse situations? How many people suffer daily without us knowing? And how many more people will have to suffer before we begin to care, our opinions ceasing to be cloaked by prejudice and fear? When will Australians see refugees not as 'queue jumpers' or 'illegals', or people who threaten their livelihoods merely by their presence in our country, but as people who deserve the choice about what religion they practice, who deserve the right to walk down the street without fear of being shot, and the ability to say that freedom is their reality.

On one point at least, there is no discrepancy. Some issues are universal – transcending race, nationality and geography. Their vote is unanimous – Brazil will win the World Cup.

These boys all seek peace, have the desire to learn and the willingness to work. What more could Australia ask of its youth?

Experience as Refugee

by Mohammad Riyadh Ali, aged 20

A dark dream left a mark in my heart, mind and soul.

It was lunchtime and our family gathered for lunch. We were not expecting anyone so when we heard the doorbell ring in a strange way, it instantly caught our attention. When my grandfather opened the door it was a shock. We could not believe it.

Some soldiers pushed their way into the house to arrest us for no reason. None of us could talk because we were still in shock. They immediately threw us out of the house and took everything of any value. We watched as this went on but could not do anything. They destroyed all our furniture and other belongings but still we didn't react. They took away my five uncles and grandfather. Only the children and the women were left behind and we were all on the street, homeless.

That day I looked left and right for the person to wipe away my tears and solve my problem. But my dad, who was the problem solver, was away. We went to my uncle's wife's house. For eight months we were running here and there, searching for my uncle, but there was no hope left.

After eight months passed they told my grandmother to come and collect their dead bodies.

After three years my dad came home. I saw the light in his eyes, which gave me new hope to live. It was here that our journey to freedom began.

Our refugee journey took us to the cold weather, and the snow on the mountains which was three feet deep. I was with a strange man, who was carrying me on his shoulders at the front, and my parents and siblings were behind me riding mules. The mule that my mother and sister were riding nearly threw them from the mountains, but my mother risked her life to save my sister. Every step we took gave us either life or death.

The war was above our heads and you could see easily the booms and rackets in front and behind. We were very frightened, and separated by some distance, but we could see each other clearly. Because of the war we forgot how hungry, and how cold the weather was. We didn't have any money, food; and our clothes were too wet from the snow.

We finally reached a border and got a little help. People gave us some food and blankets. The next morning they sent us to another border with a person who could get us through easily by his help. We passed through seven borders. Travelling from one place to another place took us one week on the mountains but at last we reached Iran's border. When we reached Iran the soldiers took us to the Red Cross. Then they took us to the refugees' camp after we finished with the Red Cross.

We stayed there for a long time. My troubles began there. I began to see things that happened to us and started having dark dreams. I screamed, fought, ran like a wild person, afraid of everybody, even my parents. I couldn't sleep at night or day. My parents took me to different doctors but there was no hope for me.

My parents did some hard labour and were paid a little money. The money was only enough to take us to Pakistan. On the way to Pakistan we were frightened by the street gangs but it was our only hope and we reached the borders safely and entered Pakistan.

The next morning we went to the UN. We applied for help and they accepted us, and gave us a green card which allowed us to stay as long as it took them to find a country which would accept us as citizens.

The problem of my health was worse. I began to walk in my sleep and fight with everyone in my family. Then one night in my sleep a holy person came into my dream and told me that I would receive help as long as I could give twenty-six Arabic characters. When I began to read them, the holy person began to scream from the pain, because he took half of my sickness and there it stopped. There was only silence for a few days of my life. Then the dreams stopped.

Ten years in Pakistan the UN made us stay, which was the hardest thing ever. We weren't allowed to go out with friends, or out of the school due to the violence all around. Even young boys carried knives or guns. So it wasn't safe for us to live in Pakistan. During our eleventh year in Pakistan we were told that the Australian government had offered us citizenship. Then when we left Pakistan we couldn't believe our eyes and our luck. Now we have started a new life and now have new hope.

Lucie's Story:
Love and Danger

by Gabriel M Courtney, aged 11

I think if your life's in danger, and especially if you really love in such a courageous way, as Jan did love me, then it sort of gives you strength to do the almost impossible. Lucie Pollack-Langford

Lucie Pollack-Langford, the lady I interviewed, was a refugee not once, but twice in her long and fascinating life. Not only that, the first time, after experiencing terrible dangers, Lucie became a refugee in disguise in the very country that was persecuting her own people, because this was the only way she could save her own life. While Lucie told me her story, it seemed to take hold of me. It was like I was her and these things were happening to me. Altogether, I found that Lucie is an amazing person, and I feel extremely lucky to have met someone like her.

Lucie Pollack-Langford is Jewish. She was born before the Second World War in the city of Prague, in former Czechoslovakia, which is now the Czech Republic. Lucie told me that there is a saying in Prague, that every baby born there is born with a violin in their cradle. Jokingly, she said that she was born with a gramophone record in hers. She remembers that when she was just a little girl, she had a small gramophone which she used to wind up and dance to the music for hours and hours. Lucie's life in Australia has always been involved with music, which she said might be because of the 'gramophone record in her cradle'.

During World War II, the German Nazi Party took away the property, jobs, and eventually the lives of over six million Jewish people. They kept records of every Jewish person, who could be identified by the yellow star they were forced to wear. So when the time came to take Lucie's family from their home, it was easy to organise them to go to a local 'exit point' as they called it, which was a school in a place called Terezin. At that time, Lucie was only fifteen years old. She and her family were taken to Poland to a concentration camp called Sovivor, upon which everyone was separated into those who could work and those who could not. Those who could not work were shot shortly after. Luckily, Lucie was able to work. She was taken to a place called Sawin, which was one of many small labour camps. The work was digging irrigation canals which was extremely hard labour, from which many people got sick and were sent to death camps for 'orderly disposal.' By this time Lucie was sixteen and loved dancing. The prisoners were allowed to have a concert, at which Lucie met a Polish Christian engineer named Jan Hensel, who, though not a prisoner himself, was forced by the Germans to work at the camp. They fell in love. Lucie and Jan spent a year in a very dangerous situation, because if they had been found out, they would have doubtlessly both been shot. They realised the only way to keep Lucie alive was to help her escape. During that year, Jan taught Lucie Polish, he fed her, and after sneaking her out of the camp, hid her in his family's home until she could escape from Poland. His family got her false documents, which said that she was a Polish Christian girl. I was happy when Lucie said she had escaped from the camp, but I was sad when she said she never saw Jan again.

Lucie went to Lublin, a city in Poland. She departed from there with a group of Christian girls on Polish transport to – of all places – Germany, where she ended up working with nuns in a Catholic hospital in the city of Soest for two years. During that time, Lucie said she had to be incredibly careful. That is how she survived for two years, until American forces came and liberated Europe. Immediately after liberation, Lucie had to stay in Germany for a little while – for a couple of years. There she worked in the High Court as an interpreter for the Control Commission of Germany as she speaks several languages – French, German, English, Polish and some Russian. Then Lucie returned to the Czech Republic, but in 1948, the Communists came to power there, and this political system threatened her freedom as an individual. So, after some time and difficulty, she managed to get out and went to England. There Lucie worked as a nurse for a year, after which, in 1950, she came to Australia.

Here in Australia, Lucie said she made the rounds of many businesses, but her skill in languages did not seem to be as sought after in this country. One day, she went into a music store named Palings. The people there said that they did not really need an interpreter or receptionist, but asked if she would like to work in their classical music department. Lucie answered, 'Ooh yes! I'd love that!' Around that time, she also did find work as an interpreter, because there were many migrants arriving in Australia. They were very eager to listen to music from their homelands, so Lucie became involved in buying foreign music recordings to supply their needs. Since then, Lucie worked for Rosestreet Records and has also managed the music lounge of Angus and Robertson bookstore. Most of Lucie's working life has been involved with music and records, just as her life began in Prague! She said: 'I hope that in some way I contributed towards the cultural life of Australia.' Lucie now also gives lectures at universities about her experiences during the war.

Lucie's mother and step-father died during the war, but she did find two of her cousins, Martin and Veran and their parents, who are still alive now. They also had a very interesting escape, which involved the Nazis 'bartering' to be paid for releasing the European relatives of rich American Jews. However, usually by the time that such deals were made, the relatives were already dead. Luckily, Lucie's relatives were sent to Switzerland, and their lives were saved.

Lucie works presently as a guide at the Sydney Jewish Museum. One day, a Polish Jewish woman came to visit the museum as she had some task to do for SBS Broadcasting. She and Lucie began a conversation, and it turned out that she was soon to visit Poland. They became friends, and later the lady rang Lucie from Poland with exciting news. Lucie had given Jan's name and details to her friend, and she had found his family. Unfortunately Jan had died in 1994, when Lucie herself had been visiting Prague in only 1993! Lucie began to correspond with Jan's family. Then, her husband Peter, who is Dutch, reminded her about 'Righteous Among the Nations.' Righteous Among the Nations is a special department of the Israeli government in Jerusalem, which considers the cases of efforts made by non-Jewish persons – Gentiles – who helped Jews during the war. This department declared Jan and his sister Danuta to be 'Righteous Gentiles Among the Nations'.. There is an important ceremony for this declaration, so in 1999 Lucie travelled to Poland, where she met with Jan's family. She became close friends 'like sisters' with his widow, and stayed in her home, where Jan had lived for forty years! His family took her all around Poland, as well as back to the camp where they had been together. Lucie said it was a surreal situation, but an absolutely amazing experience.

When I asked her, Lucie said that she loves living in Australia, and she likes to go overseas on holidays to visit relatives. But, she added, Australia is now home! At the beginning I said Lucie is an amazing person, just like her story. Now she is writing a book about her life, which she hopes will be made into a movie. Then everyone will be lucky, like me, to hear her story too.

Broken Hearts

by Ariel Smith, aged 12

Imagine, you've got no nationality, nowhere to live, no money, no country wants you and on top of it all you've got no family. Michael has experienced all of the above. He was born in Baghdad, Iraq in 1975. He had Iraqi citizenship, his father had Iraqi citizenship and his mother had Iraqi citizenship. His ancestors were Kurds. In 1980 he was five years old and had no siblings. His mother and he were deported to Iran from Iraq in 1980. His mother died five months later in a refugee camp. He still to this day does not know how she died, only that she is buried in Tehran. An Iranian family took him in, they were not his relatives and never legally adopted him. The authorities gave him a green card (a green card is issued to a refugee in Iran from Iraq). The family gave him a new name, however his green card held his true name. He was not allowed to go to school or get a job, the family kept him at home and had him working as a full time servant doing household chores. He did manage to learn to read and write from a neighbour who was a teacher. He was approximately twelve or thirteen years old when they started and got taught for the next seven or eight years. He lived with this family until 1999. The family was violent and treated him badly. When he was eight years old they burnt his hand with a cigarette and broke his nose. The beatings were a regular thing over the years for any small excuse, for example if they were not happy with the way he had cleaned, or if some item was broken or lost he would be blamed and beaten. In June 1999 the lady of the house had broken the TV by knocking it off the stand. The wife and children had beaten him with a belt buckle to force the false confession to the husband that he had broken the TV. He could not report them to the police because he was a green card holder and the authorities would not assist him. A green card holder does not have any rights. He feared that if he went to the authorities he would be sent back to Iraq as Iranians were sending Iraqis back to Iraq, even green card holders. They were also deporting Afghans. His neighbour suggested that he go to the Bezisti (Ministry of social welfare) but he thought they would say he was an adult and he should leave. He was afraid to leave as he had no skills to live on his own. He told Mr Zaree that he wanted to leave and that he might go to the Bezisti and complain, he told him that his wife broke the TV, not him. Mr Zaree realised he was serious so he suggested that he go to Tehran and stay at his company office. He was told to do the cleaning during the day and odd jobs. He was not paid, the man would give him money for food but not for his work. He did this for two years.

There was an engineer who also worked there. He said that Michael had no future, no identity, no documents and he could not work legally. He had seen Afghans and Iraqis being forced into trucks and being taken to the border on TV. The engineer felt sorry for him and paid a smuggler to help him leave. The engineer paid for the passport and then his ticket. He gave up his green card and left with the smuggler. He boarded the plane; he was instructed he would meet someone in Malaysia. They then went to Indonesia by boat illegally and remained there for two weeks before coming to Australia by boat. It took twelve days and Michael has been incarcerated since. With fewer rights than a serial killer.

My name is Ariel Smith. I am twelve years of age. I am an activist for refugees, attending weekly meetings with the local Refugee Action Collective. I attend rallies, forums and information stalls at local markets. I have spoken twice on radio recently regarding the refugee situation. My mother and I are currently offering support to this detainee. We have developed a strong bond – he and I are like brothers now. Having already been refused a temporary protection visa, his chances are very slim. Even if deported he will still owe the Federal Government over $35,000! This is the cost of his incarceration.

Far from Home:
Thinh's Journey to Safety

by Tita Tran, aged 12

It happened twenty years ago but I remember it all as if it happened just yesterday. These experiences changed my life forever. Many people wouldn't believe what I suffered. It still makes me cry and it hurts me just to think about it. I have kept it to myself for all these years, but today, I would like to tell everybody. I hope doing this will take away the pain and sorrow that I have kept to myself for so long and help my soul to heal. I also hope that by doing this more people will realise that not everybody is lucky and not everybody can have a totally happy life.

My name is Nguyen Tan Thinh.

It was the year 1980 just after North Vietnam took over South Vietnam. I was only nineteen years old. I attended Binh Chieu High School. I had short, straight, pitch-black hair. I was skinny and quite tall for my age. I lived in a family of nine kids, including me. I had five sisters and three brothers. I was the youngest in the family – and also the luckiest because my brothers and sisters adored and spoilt me. But when I think about what happened to me, I think I was really unlucky.

I can never forget the day I heard the news. I was walking home from school when I came across a North Vietnamese soldier. I said 'Hi' to him to be polite and he asked to see my school books. He said he wanted to see what students were taught nowadays. I stood there quietly as he looked through my books. I suddenly remembered something as he flipped through my writing book. The original flag of Vietnam was still in this book. I prayed he wouldn't notice it but he did – I guess this was my bad day. I expected him to at least hit me but he ripped the whole page out instead.

Then he said, 'You know now that North Vietnam has taken over and the new flag is the one you must have in your book! You know the one with the yellow star and red background? Not the old flag with the yellow background and three red stripes! I thought you were a clever boy; I almost considered that I should not send you to war with Cambodia but now, you *will* help fight the war for us. From now on, you are no longer a student. I expect to see you tomorrow morning at Trai Bien Hoa!'

I knew that Trai Bien Hoa was a place where they trained soldiers. I tried telling him that my family was too poor to buy me a new book, so I had to keep the old book with the old flag. I knew the North Vietnamese did not like the old flag, so I should not have had the old flag any more. But he would not listen to me at all, so, defeated, I just continued walking home with a sick feeling in the bottom of my stomach.

I was sad. I knew that my family would be very sad and worried for me. I had seen them react that way when they found out that all of my brothers were expected to go to war. Should I just tell them the bad news straight away when I got home, or should I slowly bring it up during a conversation? I felt like crying but I stopped myself. Someone might see me. After all I am a boy and boys are only expected to bleed, not shed tears. That was an old saying that meant that boys should be tough and not soft or able to show any emotion.

When I arrived home my mother was worried and asked me lots of questions.

'How was school Thinh? Why did you take so long to get home? Was everything all right? You didn't hang out with friends or have a fight, did you?'

I just couldn't answer her. I told her that there was nothing to worry about. I told her that I was old enough to look after myself. My mother started yelling at me because she knew that the North Vietnamese soldiers patrolled the streets and she also knew that I still had the old Vietnamese flag in my book. She was worried that the soldiers would beat me for this but she just couldn't afford a new book.

Some people would think this is a silly reason for anyone to beat you but North Vietnam soldiers were strict and bad tempered. They would attack you if you did something they didn't like.

I shouted at my mother and told her not to worry but I was worried myself. However, I didn't let it show. If I had she would have been even more worried than she was. My mother was shocked; I usually never did anything rude to my elders. She looked really hurt and sad. I suddenly felt ashamed of myself; I shouldn't have been rude to my mum. I shouldn't have told her not to worry and I was old enough to look after myself. That is considered as answering back and being cheeky to your elders and to Vietnamese people that is *extremely* rude if you are a child.

My mother started yelling. I didn't quite understand what she was saying. I must have got caught in my own horrible thoughts while she rambled on. I decided that it was better if she knew the truth.

'I'm sorry, mother. I shouldn't have tried to hide things. I shouldn't have answered back *or* raised my voice at you, either.'

My mother must have seen the sad, worried look on my face because she calmed down straight away.

'Tell me what happened, Thinh,' she replied soothingly.

I told my mother about what had happened during my walk home but I stopped when I got to the part about the flag. I just couldn't carry on.

'Go on, Thinh, what happened? Don't worry, do go on,' my mother encouraged me.

I nodded and finished telling her the story. I told her that the soldier said that I would have to help fight the war against Cambodia. I apologised to my mother and told her that I should have listened to her and ripped the page out. I also shouldn't have lied about what happened but I couldn't help it. I knew how sad she would be when she found out that I had to go to war.

There was a silence for a few moments. I could tell my mum was really sad and shocked. She sobbed.

'What am I going to do, Thinh? All your brothers are expected to go to war! Now you are going as well! There is a very slim chance that all of you will survive. What am I going to do?'

I tried to comfort her but I couldn't. There was nothing I could do so I went into my bedroom, lay on my bed and thought about what I should do.

After a while an idea hit me. I could simply run away and come back *after* the war had finished! Or maybe I could even settle in another country!

I didn't sleep well that night. I was worried. I planned to leave home at one o'clock the next morning. I accidentally over-slept and woke up at one-thirty. I quickly packed and wrote a goodbye letter to my family. It read:

'*Dear Family,*

I am sorry, but I have to leave. I will go to another country and settle down. That way I can escape going to war. I will come back when the war has ended. If I really enjoy the new country, maybe we can all move there. Please send me letters and money, although I will not be able to reply except when I need to tell you where I am. At least by doing this, I have a better chance of surviving and coming back. Once again, I'm sorry. Don't worry: I can take care of myself. I'll miss you all, but I have to go.

Love, Nguyen Tan Thinh.'

I left the letter on the kitchen table and set off to find the perfect country. I knew the journey was going to be tiring and dangerous. I got on a truck that was going to Cambodia. I knew it was heading that way because I had asked politely with a casual interest. Luckily for me the truck driver was lonely. He had to deliver things all the time so when someone talked to him he would tell them anything.

I soon found out that the truck was transporting bags of cement and lots of bricks. I thought this was the best way to get to Cambodia without having to pay or walk. I could easily hide behind the bricks and use the bags to sleep on. I felt bad for doing something dishonest, and there was a chance of getting the driver fired if they happened to find me in his truck. But I just pushed the thought away, thinking that I could leave him a little bit of money when I left.

Just as I got into the truck I got scared, because I knew that there would be no way of turning back after this. Going to a country I was meant to fight against was going to be very dangerous but I had to take the chance, because that is the easiest way to get through to Thailand and safety. From Thailand I had planned in my head to somehow travel to Australia or America.

The journey on the truck was rough. I closed my eyes for a while. A bang woke me up. I didn't have a watch, but I had brought a small clock with me. It was eleven PM. I had been asleep five whole hours! That was dangerous – I could have been caught. I hadn't even asked the driver for a ride. I had just climbed into the back of the truck because if I had asked him he would have said no, and if he had said yes, he would probably have charged me a fortune.

I opened the door at the back of the truck and looked around. I was at a petrol station. The bang must have been from the slamming of the front door. Nobody was around, so I climbed out.

I hid behind a bush and looked around. Where was I? I caught sight of a banner saying Ha Tien Karaoke. I must be in

Ha Tien. For once I felt lucky. Ha Tien was near the border of Cambodia.

I got back into the truck and hid myself carefully. I hoped to get some more sleep as soon as the driver got back. I would get off the truck as soon as it had passed through the border of Cambodia. I hoped that the truck would not be searched. Soon afterwards I heard the driver return and we began our journey to the Cambodian border.

I was lucky. The truck was searched but during the ride bricks and cement had fallen on top of me. They hid me from view and the soldiers were too lazy to check through the pile. The bricks and bags were heavy. While I was asleep I didn't feel a thing, but my body ached and I had some bruises and cuts afterwards.

I still felt nervous, even though I had not been caught. Any time now the truck might stop and unload, which meant I had a chance of being discovered. I was lucky, once again lucky. The truck did not stop until early next day and then the driver only stopped to fill the petrol tank.

I slowly opened the door and got out. I left five hundred thousand dong for the driver. I also left a note saying, 'Thanks for the ride.' Then I ran away as fast as I could. When I thought I was a safe distance away I stopped and rested. After a while I went around to ask directions. I was lucky that I was taught Cambodian and Thai in school. Some people looked at me angrily and walked away.

I soon found out from a nice old man that I was only eight days away from the border of Thailand. I thanked him and set off to find some food.

I bought things I needed for the journey. I also wrote a letter to my family and sent it. I said that I was heading to Thailand. When I was ready I set off.

I was really tired for the following days because I had very few breaks. I wanted to get to Thailand quickly. I soon became thin, weak and dirty. I don't think my own mother would have recognised me in the state that I was in. Being safe and alive kept me going. On the eighth day I reached the border. It was early in the morning. I hoped they would let me through.

When I reached the two soldiers who were guarding the border I stopped. They asked me where I was going and why. I told them I was going to Thailand because I was running away from my country, Vietnam. They nodded and then started talking to each other quietly so that I couldn't hear. They then turned toward me. One of them threatened to shoot me and the other stripped me of all my money, food, valuables and clothes. They left me with only my old shirt and pants. After that they let me go. I hurried away but several metres further on they stopped me again. I could hear them arguing. It seemed that they had planted bombs under the ground and had expected them to explode and kill me. I was horrified that a person could do that to another human being.

I was soon locked away in a cell. The cell was cold, damp, dirty and smelly. I also saw a few rats crawling around in the corner. I was fed only rice and was only allowed salt water to drink. Sometimes they would let me out to find vegetation to eat. I never tried running away because the soldiers always accompanied me. The only vegetation I could find to eat was grass, bark and leaves. The soldiers would enjoy this and would laugh at me crawling around looking for something to eat. After that they would lock me up again.

At midnight every night they would wake me up and splash freezing water on me. It was so cold I would become numb. I tried not going to sleep so as not to endure this torture, but I was too tired and weak.

After they had woken me they would take me to a different room. They would tie me to the ceiling by my toes and beat me with a hard stick. The pain was unbearable even through the numbness. I couldn't help screaming loudly and crying. That would make them angry and they would hit even harder. They also told me what a baby I was.

While they were hitting me they asked me questions. They would ask me why I was here and who I was. They thought I was a spy.

I would always reply the same way: 'I am Nguyen Tan Thinh. I live in Bien Hoa. I only came here to run away from Vietnam because I didn't want to fight in a war.'

They would never accept the answer and would just hit harder.

I always feared those times. I even put up a fight once, holding hard onto the door of my cell. But that only caused me more pain; they would get a metal pole and hit my fingers. I never tried that again. The pain was unbelievable. I never tried anything else either. I was sure anything would result in more pain and agony.

The Thai soldiers also took all the money that my family sent me. I knew because they would show me the letter and then take away the money. They never let me send anything. They said posting it was a waste of money and I might tell my family what was happening.

One day I got the courage to ask them for a pen and paper. I quietly wrote a letter to my family, asking them to help me but not to send any money. I put it in a stamped envelope, which I had hidden under the straw in my cell. Luckily they had not searched me properly when they first captured me. I bribed a soldier to send a letter for me and he agreed.

Two weeks later while I was sleeping, somebody opened my cell and dragged me out. I heard a gruff voice saying in my ear, 'You may be lucky, but if I ever find any proof that you really are a spy you will die slowly and painfully!'

I was scared. Where was I being taken now? I soon found out. I was taken out of the gaol and a letter was shoved in my hand. The guard then quickly shut the gate and walked back inside.

I opened the letter which said that my family had paid the Vietnamese Government to help me. There was a trial and I was proven innocent. I was free but I had to stay in Thailand for four years. I was paid back all the money the soldiers had taken from me. I was so happy that I jumped for joy.

During the four years in Thailand I learnt and taught English. I had a happy life. Four years later, in 1984, I left Thailand. I stowed away in a boat that transported goods, with about ten other Asian people.

We were found by a man who worked on the boat when he went to inspect the goods. We were then left at an island near Thailand. I cannot recall the name because I was never good at geography. I had no idea where the island was and knew little about where other countries were in relation to the island.

We were stranded on the island for three months and soon ran out of food and water. People couldn't help themselves. They drank water from the ocean then died soon after.

We got to a stage where people went crazy, or were so hungry that they ended up eating the dead people. I was so sad and scared, just sitting there and watching things happening in front of my eyes. I was too weak to move or do anything. I stopped myself from eating people or drinking sea water. But deep down I knew that one day I would go crazy. I prayed and hoped that we would be saved soon.

My prayers were answered because an Australian ship happened to come by and see us. The people that were left were overjoyed. There weren't many of us, only four. We all were taken to Australia.

Some people died soon after they reached Australia. Some went crazy. Some got jobs and lived happily. I was one of them: I now work in a factory putting goods into packages. I live alone and am now forty-one. My dad has died, so has my brother Hoan and sister Mai. My brother died after the war and my sister died of pneumonia. My sisters Son and Thi are also in Australia, though their journey was not rough. I see them sometimes. The rest of my family are still in Vietnam. One day I will help them migrate to Australia, so our family can reunite. But for now, I will send letters and money. I really miss them.

I do feel a little better now that I have told everyone my story. I hope you will understand and appreciate what you have. Not all people are born in a rich land. Not all people can live easily. Not all have happy lives. I am one of those unfortunate people. I hope by telling you this story you will understand the suffering some people have to endure. Many of us have hidden secrets and pains from our journeys or sadness because of the loss of loved ones.

Five Months

by Katie Petrie, aged 15

My name is Keitiah. I have only been in Australia for five months, but I know it is good place. My family came from Aeritrea, because of the horrible tragedies occurring there. My father was a journalist so the government on many occasions tried to kill our family and friends. They succeeded on many occasions, causing pain and heartache for many people.

In 1994, five government soldiers locked my best friend, Mieraf, in a house and set it on fire. I was the only one who saw it. The soldiers held my hands behind my back and hit me with their guns until my body was limp from exhaustion and pain. Although my vision was blurry, the soldiers held my head up so I had to watch the rest of the house crumble to ash. Mieraf's screams had stopped while the soldiers were beating me. I knew he was dead and cried myself to sleep in the gutter.

The soldiers found me in the morning. I was in the same place they had left me. I believe they suspected that I was my father's daughter (we were well known in Aeritrea). They stripped my clothes off and hit me with their guns until I was unconscious. I awoke with my hands and feet tied. I was still naked. I noticed that I was outside my front door. A note had been wired through my skin with two pieces of rusty metal. I kicked on my front door until my father answered my pounding. He swept me up in his arms, soaking me with his tears of relief. My mother carefully removed the note from my stomach. It read, 'You must be out of the country this time next week, or we will kill your family.'

We had received many notes like this, but nothing had happened. This note scared me as it seemed real, the soldiers had never been this violent before. My mother and father stayed up late talking about the situation. In the morning, much to my anguish, they announced that we would be staying in Aeritrea.

Two weeks and three days later the soldiers locked us in our house and set it on fire. We sat in the house until the soldiers left. Although the soldiers set fire to our house, we were not burnt. Our friends saw the house burning, but we were safe. Many people we know have attributed our survival to a miracle performed by God. There was no fire damage on the house, so we continued living there.

The soldiers tried many other times to harm our family, but weren't successful. On a normal Saturday morning, the soldiers opened fire on a busy market place, shooting everyone they saw and wasting bullets on fruit and animals. They knocked over tables, stalls and carts. On that same morning my two brothers went to the market to buy some chickens. They were two of the few survivors of the massacre.

I was saved from death another time, but only to have three of my friends murdered. We were walking through the town when a group of soldiers recognised me; the only excuse they needed to kill more innocent citizens. They pinned my friend, Sari, to the ground, and while she was still struggling they shot her eighteen times, using all their bullets. They grabbed my second friend and pinned him to the ground, now covered in Sari's blood. One of the soldiers had a flimsy pocket knife and as they had run out of bullets they decided to use the knife. They stabbed him several times until his eyes stopped blinking. They stabbed both his eyeballs, just because they could. The soldiers grabbed my third friend who was screaming and wailing. One soldier kicked her in the head and told her to shut up. Before the soldiers started mutilating their third victim, one took a swipe at my stomach with the knife. I tried to avoid it, but couldn't. The knife plunged down into my muscles, causing instant pain. Seeing me writhe in pain, the soldiers laughed and jeered at me. They turned back to Nyanchieu, my only remaining friend. The soldiers stabbed with such aggression and for so long, the flimsy knife blade snapped. At this the soldiers laughed, kicked me and once again left me on the street.

I stayed in the same spot for two hours, wailing and mourning the death of my friends. The pins and needles in my feet and legs were so bad, I couldn't walk properly. I dragged my limp lower body home, still crying. When I got home my parents were waiting for me with my brothers and sister. They had decided we were leaving Aeritrea the following week.

When I stepped off the plane in Australia, the first thing I noticed was how everything seemed paved, there was no dirt anywhere. The airport was huge and I could see grass in a distant field. I felt as if a huge weight had been lifted off my shoulders. You may think I am a coward for leaving, but I have been through so much in such a short time, I can hardly explain it all. We are safer here in Australia and I hope one day my other friends are able to come and live here too.

Even though I have had to learn a new language, and I miss my home and grieve for my friends, it is far outweighed by the peace and security we feel living in this country. I am going to school and have made many new friends. In some ways Australia does remind me of home.

THE WAVES
TO FREEDOM

'Mummy, I don't want to go on another boat ever
again. I don't want Daddy to die again.'

Waleed Alkhazrajy: Perserverance Personified

by Yasmin Aleem, aged 17

Can you imagine having to leave your homeland, your family, friends, career and life, for fear of being killed by the government? Can you imagine travelling through 1700 kilometres of desert, with nothing but the clothes on your back? Can you imagine being detained for ten months in a foreign land, and given little opportunity to prove your worth? Maybe you can't, but many can. In fact they don't have to imagine it, because for individuals like Waleed Alkhazrajy, these events actually happened.

Waleed was born in Iraq, where he was raised as a Muslim and still practises his religion. Though now an Australian citizen, his path was far from easy.

Waleed's story starts in 1995, in Iraq, where he worked as a doctor. The Iraqi government had previously announced that all those who deserted the military would be branded with a cross on their forehead or have their ears cut off. This barbaric decree was published on Friday, notifying Waleed that this would be one of his duties on Monday. Waleed's reason for becoming a doctor was to treat illnesses. This decree was a complete contradiction of what he believed in, so he refused to carry out any acts of mutilation. Consequently, Waleed fled the country that Saturday morning, in blatant defiance of the Iraqi government. This meant that Waleed was himself liable to major persecution and his defiance punishable by death.

Waleed left for Jordan after fleeing Iraq and, using all available methods of transport, travelled through the Syrian Desert. For us, it's hard to imagine just what kind of physical, psychological and emotional stress Waleed was under. He stayed in Jordan for a year, but did so without ever having a real identity because he did not have any official documents. Had he been caught by either the Iraqi or Jordanian governments, he would have been sent home to face death. Waleed was in 'limbo', as he was also unable to apply to the United Nations High Commission for Refugees, because it was under surveillance by Iraqi intelligence; anyone who approached that organisation would be traced and probably killed or transported back to Iraq. Anyone in a similar situation would feel compelled to resort to extreme measures.

Waleed's family paid nearly A$30,000 to people-smugglers, to ensure he reached Australia. This amount is not too much for the wealthy, and the truth of the matter is that 90 per cent of oppressed, articulate Iraqis are rich enough to pay this sum. Sadly, such information is not reported, because it does not correspond with the image that the Australian government has. The government has created an image which depicts the majority of Iraqis coming for economic reasons, and those here are wealthy and thus described as greedy, selfish queue-jumpers, because they are apparently preventing other deserving immigrants the chance.

Waleed says that those who have the money to come simply do not have the means to apply in the manner the Australian government would prefer: '. . . we had to find other ways of coming, otherwise we would have died.'

Waleed placed his life in the hands of people-smugglers, who are: 'from the dark side of this world; people that you can't trust with your life or your money.' The journey took two weeks; starting from Jordan, flying to Kuala Lumpur, crossing the border over the sea to Indonesia, then to East Timor. The group that Waleed was travelling with then boarded a small, wooden fisherman's vessel and ended up near Ashmore Reef, off-shore in North-West Western Australia.

Why would a university graduate, who had lived a life of relative luxury, choose to come to Australia in this manner? Why would an educated man, who cannot swim, decide to spend two weeks in a leaking, wooden fisherman's boat with fifteen others? The answer is simple, but profoundly disturbing. Waleed concluded that he was certain to die anyway – at the hands of the Iraqi government, the people-smugglers or while crossing the sea. His attitude was: 'Either you make it or you don't.' I do not know anyone else who can say that they have been in similar situations. Situations of such desperation are the cause of erratic actions; this can be seen in Waleed's decision to take a chance, to reach what he perceived to be a land of justice and democracy.

Sadly, the image of Australia being the country of 'a fair go' is false. This was not what Waleed was met with when he arrived at Ashmore Reef in late 1996. He was immediately detained for ten months: 'for political reasons'. Waleed accepted that there were many motives for the government to detain him, one of them being that, by stopping people from coming, Australia would no longer be seen as an 'easy target'. Another motive is that, at the time, the Iraqi government had signed a deal worth $50 million with Australia to trade wheat in return for the Food for Oil program. This was organised through the UN and our government did not want it ruined by accepting immigrants, especially those the Iraqi government was looking for. There was pressure to send the refugees back, otherwise the deal would be forfeited. Australia was, no doubt, putting trade before principles, and Waleed, along with the others who arrived with him, were victims of this morally-indefensible practice.

At the Port Hedland Detention Centre, Waleed was subject to completely inconsistent treatment, '. . . showing us a hard time so that we will tell the others that are to follow not to come. We were very patient to tolerate that treatment; we thought *Is this the last chapter in our story of suffering?* and if it is, then we will tolerate it, just as we have tolerated years of persecution in Iraq.'

After one month that the refugees were told that they would meet with Immigration officials. During that time, Waleed and the others were kept in tight security. They could only see the sun for ten minutes in the morning and in the afternoon, (smoking time for smokers), but all used that as an excuse to get out: 'otherwise we will be locked up the whole day.'

Injustice did not end there. Before his meeting with Immigration authorities, Waleed and the others were provided with a solicitor, to present their cases. The solicitor was formerly a priest; his first question was: ' Why did you come to Australia; this is not a Muslim country?' He treated all matters on a racial basis. The group then spent five months waiting for the ultimate decision from Immigration. Their applications were refused; after hearing this, the group changed solicitor. 'We approached the Red Cross and they provided us with the names and contacts of some people who are genuine refugee advocates.' The Refugee Casework Association was able to help Waleed and the others, and two months later they received their refugee protection visas; they had finally been granted refugee status!

After leaving the detention centre in late 1997, Waleed studied for one year, then, in October 1998, took the Australian Medical Exam, a test that all overseas-trained doctors must sit for their qualifications to be recognised in Australia, regardless of background or country of birth. Waleed's results were very promising; he achieved 82 per cent, which ranked him as the second-highest candidate of 317, Australia-wide.

He then worked in the Frankston Hospital, in the emergency department, first as a junior doctor, but was soon promoted to the position of registrar, after his talent was recognised. His medical interests were to specialise in anaesthetics and so he applied, and was accepted, for the South Australian training program, supported by the Australian and New Zealand College of Anaesthetists. Waleed has worked in two South Australian hospitals, and is currently posted as registrar at the Royal Adelaide Hospital.

Waleed now tries to help any junior doctors with exam preparation, as he was helped by those senior to him.

Waleed is happily married to Nicole, whom he met in Australia. Nicole is a radiographer, and both Waleed and Nicole have made many friends here in Adelaide. In January 2002, they bought a house in Unley. They are settled and happy with their work and social lives.

Waleed still has strong opinions about world issues, especially those related to immigration. Those who apply for refugee status were not only victims of politics in their own countries, but were also faced with politics upon arriving in Australia. They are from specific racial and religious groups and, while it is not articulated, sadly, this is one of the reasons. Waleed knows that such people are not at all a threat to the freedom of this country; they simply want to live a quiet, peaceful life.

In Waleed's opinion, Australian detention centres are becoming worse. Now, emergency workers have limited access, along with the media. The new Port Augusta Detention Centre is not guarded by razor-wire fences, like others of its kind, but instead by a six metre-high electric fence. Waleed emphasises that: 'erecting an electric fence just increases the humiliation for these people.'

In light of the many protests staged around the country, Waleed claims to have a certain respect for the protesters. He feels that the majority of Australians 'have chosen to be blind' to the issue. He believes that '99 per cent of people choose to do nothing, while just a few people do something.'

Australia now supports those world powers which have decided to proclaim that they are 'defending the freedom' of Western countries, while single-handedly preventing many from accessing the same freedom of which we speak so fondly. Double standards are present everywhere. History proves that not all actions mirror the clean-cut image which is portrayed. A jumbo-jet was blown up while flying over Lockerbie, Scotland in 1989. Most of the passengers were either American or Scottish, and Libya was blamed for the incident, recognised as an act of terror. Four hundred died; they were all innocent. Libya was pressured to pay $10 million for every death. Yet recently, in Afghanistan, when a US missile hit a wedding party, killing forty and injuring fifty, the price of life was not considered to be as high. The United States accepted responsibility, yet only $200 was paid to the families of those who died and $75 to those injured. How much are people worth in different countries?

Waleed is a truly admirable person. I have the utmost respect for this man, who has endured much; with perseverance he has achieved more that anyone could have expected. His story shows how some people have had to fight to become Australians, and how this fight has been tough, but hopefully worth it. 'I believe that Australia is a safe country and I am lucky to be here. Sometimes I wonder about being in another safe country, whether I would have been treated better, but Australia is a wonderful country.'

I hope that his story is sufficiently moving to prompt concern within the Australian community about the treatment of refugees. I believe that Waleed should be commended for his devotion to his aims, and his strength of character which has, no doubt, aided him in becoming the remarkable person he is: 'You never know who is going to be lucky to get out and establish themselves, as I have done. I think it all depends on luck,' but Waleed has largely made his own luck.

The Waves to Freedom:
The Story of Nga-Huynh Diep

by Gracia Diep, aged 15

Vietnam today is a vibrant and thriving country that is populated with people who hold brave smiles on their faces despite their country's brutal and depressing history. However, a long time ago Vietnam's atmosphere was quite a different story. Communist parties were to come and strip away everything that was precious in Vietnam from its people. The Vietnamese were forced to live without any freedom either under the tough supervision of the communist party or in a re-education camp. The only happiness that these people had was the hope of escaping the country to have another chance at freedom in another land. Nga-Huynh was only twenty-one years of age when her family risked their lives to escape Vietnam.

This is her story.

The white building lay in the small town of Bên Tra. To the local people, it was an old run down building that had been abandoned. However, on 8th June 1979 the place held more than four hundred scared and desperate people who were waiting for their ticket to freedom.

Nga-Huynh sat stiffly with her mother and father and waited, like everybody else, for the smugglers to organise the boat that they would use to escape. Nightfall came and the smuggler told the crowd to quickly assemble in a single line so they could all walk down to the boat in an orderly fashion. Nga-Huynh solemnly followed the smuggler's directions and moved towards the boat. She didn't dare to speak, as one loud voice could attract the attention of a nearby communist party. When she reached the boat and was allocated her spot, she sat down and crossed her legs. This was the position she had to remain in for most of the seven nights. As Nga and her family were on the very bottom deck of the boat, the atmosphere was extremely stuffy and she found it hard to breathe. Nga's parents were nearby and they told her not to worry, as this was the start of their journey to freedom. Nga was still very optimistic about her family's chance of survival.

The first two nights of the boat trip were very tense as the boat still had a very high risk of being spotted by a communist boat that was out at sea. The first night, Nga slept soundly as she was dreaming of the new life that would await her if she survived this boat trip.

By the third day of the trip things hadn't improved. Nga started to feel the first pangs of starvation and thirst, as there was hardly a drop of drinking water left from her family's ration. She had also been seasick a number of times throughout the day as the boat started to take on rougher waters and combat the harsh storm that was brewing over the South China Sea.

Later on that day Nga's father shook her awake and said, 'We've lost everything, Nga, including our photos,' he paused and wiped away a few tears before continuing. 'They've just thrown away all of our luggage to help lessen the load on the boat. Nga, the boat is starting to slowly fall apart. They have to do everything they can to prevent it from sinking. Nga, promise me that if I die you won't forget my face or your mother's.'

Nga realised that the boat probably had a few more days left before it would sink. She settled back against the wall and waited, like the rest of the passengers on board, to die.

The next morning Nga's mother shook her awake and told her that a man had taken his own life by jumping overboard during the night because he couldn't stand the conditions that they were in anymore. Nga was dazed and shocked. Another woman had jumped overboard meaning to die but her husband had dragged her out of the water. Suddenly, Nga heard a loud scream and a naked woman appeared and started pounding the wooden floorboards of the ship screaming: 'God take me away. God get me out of here. I want to go. I want to go.'

The elderly woman who was sitting next to Nga said, 'That woman's been possessed by the water spirits, her mind belongs to them now.'

The screaming woman was the one who had jumped overboard but was then rescued by her husband. Nga, trembling with fright, turned back to look out of the small window and wondered whether those water spirits might come and turn her mad as well. She had already contemplated that she would rather die out at sea than at the hands of the communists back home. Nga closed her eyes and tried to fall asleep.

It was early morning and Nga awoke to a cold and painfully numbing sensation that was covering her legs and buttocks. She looked down and realised that during the night water had leaked in through the floorboards, and the whole deck was now flooded with waist deep water.

'We're going to die.' Nga whispered to herself and wiped away the tears that were falling into the seawater that was numbing her body.

At night, the first few drops of rain sounded against the sides of the boat. Quickly Nga grabbed a few old tins and joined the many others on board in catching the rainwater that would become her family's drinking water for the next few days. She was glad that it had rained that night as her parents were both becoming weak, and needed all the water they could get. She helped her mother, who had become extremely faint. 'Mother, please drink some. I don't want you to die,' Nga sobbed. 'I feel like I'm dead already,' replied her mother, weakly sipping the water.

The next day Nga realised that many people on deck had already started to prepare for their death as their hope of survival was almost gone. The boat had started to fall apart even more and the water had risen up to her chest. She saw parents holding onto their small children weeping, the elderly closing their eyes awaiting the horrible fate that was to come, lovers holding onto each other and caressing each other's faces for perhaps the very last time.

The early rays of dawn started to appear as Nga slowly opened her eyes. She glanced out of the small window nearby and suddenly spotted a tiny green speck in the distance that was starting to emerge out of the horizon.

'I see land! I see land!' she screamed as she shook her parents and those around her awake.

The rest of the deck was soon awake and becoming excited as their hope for freedom was near.

It took another twelve hours before they would reach the land. During that time, Nga could not take her eyes away from the green speck, as she feared that it would be gone if she looked away. By night the first few signs of the land started to appear, lights, people, cars but most importantly freedom. Nga happily drifted to sleep.

'Wake up Nga, We're here!' cried her father. Nga woke up and quickly followed the crowd that was trying to squeeze out of the tiny door. She stepped out of the boat and admired the surroundings; she felt a cool breeze against her face and knew that she had made it through the hard journey to freedom. She could feel the sun roasting her pale skin and felt a wave of happiness wash over her for the first time since they left Vietnam.

After they settled into their cabins on this Malaysian island, Nga and the other Vietnamese headed toward the main hall in the village to have their evening meal. Having not eaten for almost eight consecutive days, Nga ate her bowl of rice, savouring every last grain. *This is the best meal I've ever had*, she thought to herself. She was relieved to find that both her parents were eating properly and neither of them was seriously ill, unlike some of the other adults on board. Nga and her family stayed at the small village for eleven days before being transported by army trucks to a nearby harbour. When they reached the harbour they were told to get on board a large ship, that would then take them to an official refugee camp in an island named Pulau PaPan.

'Mummy, I don't want to go on another boat ever again. I don't want Daddy to die again,' said a little boy, that was standing next to Nga. The boy's mother, who was now a widow, tearfully told her son that this ship would take them to a better place, where he could play with his toys again and go to school. Nga felt herself getting teary and held tightly onto both her parents' hands as she boarded the large Malaysian ship.

When she was on the ship, Nga smelt a nauseous odour that smothered over the atmosphere on board. She quickly ran to the side of the ship and joined many others in vomiting, as the odour had all been too much for her.

After one day the ship arrived at the island. Nga noticed that the island was very beautiful and happily stayed at the camp for nine months. During this time the Red Cross came and delivered clothing, food, blankets to all the refugees, and Nga felt very grateful to receive such generous support by these people.

After five months, Nga and her family received news from the High Commission of Australia that they were due to be interviewed for refugee status in Australia. Nga felt a little nervous but extremely happy as she was going to be reunited with her sister, who had already fled to Australia from Vietnam one year before. At the interview the family was told that Nga's sister was offering to sponsor them to Australia.

'We're going to see her,' cried her parents happily hugging each other. Nga spent the rest of that night celebrating with the friends she had made at the refugee camp.

A few months later, Nga boarded her first flight, which was

to Australia. She settled into her seat comfortably and gave a reassuring smile to both her parents. As the plane started to take off, she closed her eyes and for the first time ever she felt free.

Today, Nga-Huynh is a happily married, working woman with two daughters. She lives in Melbourne and has found life in Australia very pleasant and would even call it her 'home'. However, she would like to go back to Vietnam one day to see her old house and what has happened to the country since she left it in 1979. Nga-Huynh sacrificed a lot for a chance at freedom and has come out maintaining her strong character. The experiences of her escape from Vietnam haven't weakened her at all; they have made her into an even stronger person.

To Be Someone . . .

by Bojana Bokan, aged 18

That morning of late summer 1991, at the bottom of the stairs in our building, I cried, for I had forgotten my teddy bear. My father went back while my mother was comforting me. When I had the teddy bear in my arms again, I told him that I was sorry for leaving him and that it would not happen again.

Behind us heavy doors closed loudly and we found ourselves on the street – a street I knew well, for I had spent my first six years playing there. First laugh, first tears and first steps lay there. But this time, before us was a different street, different streetlights. Whispering of rustling leaves had a different sound, and the wind didn't seem to warmly welcome us but rudely cuffed us.

On the way to the village there were too many crying children who tried to find their parents to defend them, who frenziedly were running in different directions. Among scared and uneasy faces, here and there were cynical looks and smiles on faces which moved through that stream.

Hopping onto warm grandma's lap didn't last long. We left for Bosnia where first sarcastic words met us. I didn't know the reason for that, nor do I now. We were different. My first days in school weren't happy. At lunch times I didn't run around laughing, nor would I return home full of school stories. Every now and then my brother would check on me, for others would easily pick on me. But there were times when they would pick on him and I couldn't help.

Is having only one pair of pants, not eating croissants with jam in the morning but only a thin piece of bread, speaking with a different accent, a good enough reason to humiliate someone? Someone? Too early I learned the meaning of 'no one'.

The end of that school year was long awaited. The day after receiving our reports we went back home, not to open that heavy door again but just to look at our homes from a distance. The city was divided, and our building was on the other side. We could see and even hear talk among people on that side and they could hear us. Often the two different sides made provocative jokes, not because they knew each other from before but because they were going to learn about each other. We had one thing in common: they were in our houses, and we were in somebody else's houses. There was not an answer for that. They were in our city, a city unknown to them, for that was the first time they were there, while we, whose city that was, could only look at our familiar streets.

Although we were on the other side, and we were eating only bread and cherries for three years, we were happy. All that side was like one huge family. There was no reason for thinking someone would get our words wrong, or that there was somebody who would not like the way we think. Children's laughter was full of life again. The memories of that time are still vivid. Later when I learned the meaning of 'democracy' I had the picture of that time in my head.

'All good things are not lasting for long,' people would say. Probably, in that way, they were trying to find an answer for things that happened and they could not explain why.

In the spring of 1995, jokes were not interesting or laughable any more, for they became real. After four years, sounds of hand grenade changed alarm clock once more. Even if the sky was clear, thundering could be heard, and ill-timed began. Rain of bullets didn't cause rivers to flood, but innocent children's blood to flow down the streets. Red footprints, little shoes, ripped clothes, motionless bodies covered our favourite playground. Every new lightning was followed by shrill cries. And each time when one would try to go to the shelter the raindrop would hit him.

The long time after, the ill-timed stopped, for the other side expanded to our side, by someone's sick demand. Shrill cries were resounding along red streets and we found new graves without names on each turn. Is that my cousin's or my friend's grave, or of the little neighbour's child only a few summers younger than me? Am I looking at my own grave? The Dark Age came again, and the only ray of some dim light was coming from Serbia.

The way took us to the legendary city of battle, Vukovar. But we didn't stop there for long, for we were just passing by. Not staying there for long was a good in evil, for life there brought back ugly memories of my miserable life in Bosnia.

To keep going was like living on bleakness. It was impossible to stay where we were coming from, for we were unwanted. Nor was it possible to keep going, for we were unwelcome wherever we would go. But the pathway ended in Serbia.

For all there was a place, a seat in a theatre, but not for people who came from Croatia. We were just secretly looking from outside through illicit doors at the alluring stage where everything seemed easy and beautiful. When somebody, whether an adult or a light-headed child, noticed us, they would use all in their power to lower our heads, to throw us on our knees – and not to enjoy the play. The evil could not persist and he took his final part in that drama. The play finished in late March 1999. Suddenly all of us were welcome to enter into the theatre.

Like in an earthquake, everything was shaken: houses, bridges, and people's faith in themselves and life. During the day everything was as usual, but dusk would bring uneasy feelings and the need to stay close by our house with our beloved ones. Sound of an airplane, inward whistle, voiceless peal and somebody's house was turned into a huge hole in the earth. By the morning tears on cheeks were dry, and swollen eyes stared somewhere into the distance beyond the horizon where quiet moans couldn't come. Soon it wasn't possible to make any difference between day and night. There was not only one house in flame, but many houses and tongues of flames licked the sky, leaving it yellow. The following day gave an impression of dusk, for the air was filled with grime and dense smoke, and the opposite bank of the river was inaccessible. Terror became our constant attendant, while people lost their sense of time and ability to distinguish between daylight and light given by flame. Men lost any feeling of being among people, for a man could never know when somebody would turn against him. When the stage was clear we were ready to go.

For who knows how long I held my teddy bear in my arms waiting for something, probably for some door to open just a little. Finally there was one: Australia opened a door for us.

We arrived on 24th March, 2000. The first thing I noticed was a clear lofty sky, without the dark clouds that would bring rain. Somebody told us that there are no earthquakes in Australia, and that brought us back a warm feeling around our hearts, lost in the past.

It took us eleven long years to arrive, but when we exited, door left opened and the wind was friendly. We drowned into the surroundings without leaving a blip, leaving behind that label on our foreheads.

An Interview with Ali

by Sarah-Jane Bryson, aged 16

Before me sat Ali. His black hair was cut in a style common to teenage fashion and he wore a black and red polo shirt, untucked over his jeans and boots. It was easy to assume he was the same as every other student at school; our school is extremely multi-cultural, so his heavily accented English was a part of the norm. We had been shoved into a small office, about three metres by three in size, to conduct our interview so as not to disturb the others working in the library. Gesturing at the room, Ali said, 'They had rooms in the detention centres, rooms same size as this – there were three people sleeping in there.'

Ali arrived in Australia on 1st October 1999. He left his family and friends behind in Altato in Afghanistan. Ali told me Altato was a small village and its people just tried to live their lives there, but this simple lifestyle had shattered when, a year earlier, the Taliban came. At first, some of the people in the village resisted. They were killed. Ali witnessed friends, family and community members murdered and persecuted during the time the Taliban were in Altato. Ali was sixteen years old, which placed him in danger of being recruited by the Taliban to fight. 'I had reached the age that I had to do military service and also I'd be able to carry weapons so they would take me to fight . . . so, I had to escape.'

Often when the Taliban were in the village, Ali and his father escaped to the nearby mountain and lived in the caves. Ali's mother and six siblings were left vulnerable to the Taliban, who continually ransacked the villagers' houses for belongings and money and to capture young men. One was Ali's cousin, who has never been heard from since. It was at this point that Ali's father decided to send him away, so he would not suffer the same fate as his cousin.

'Firstly, my Dad contacted his friend to prepare things for me to escape the country, so I escaped in a car and he took me across the border, into Pakistan. All smuggling, so I had to hide. In Pakistan another smuggler had prepared everything to smuggle me to Indonesia, so I come to Indonesia and not knowing that I'm travelling to Indonesia. I didn't know anything . . . the things that I was caring for was to go to a place that's safe.'

Ali spent six days in Indonesia, where eventually he was taken by boat to an island covered in graves along with many other people who, like Ali, were escaping. All Ali knew about the area was that it was away from Afghanistan and the Taliban. A week later, the Australian navy rescued him.

I sat back and stared at this person I had so recently believed to be an average student at school. There was nothing normal about the story Ali told me. As he spoke, he didn't use excessive emotion. He didn't cry when he told me about leaving his family. He said it was 'just sad, like I'm escaping for my safety . . . for my own safety . . . and leave my family like I don't care about their own safety, because they were in danger as well.' The entire time I spoke to Ali he was the figure of calmness, eyes that had seen what no sixteen-year-old should ever see and a face that had been twisted in fear while hiding in the boot of a car, being smuggled away from the only home he had ever known. It was a face of acceptance. What was done was done.

Hearing of what this boy had lived through was enough to change my entire beliefs about the refugee situation in Australia.

Until meeting Ali, my views on the refugee crisis were greatly influenced by those people I thought wise and informed on the matter. It shames me to admit that I once thought that these people seeking refuge should be sent right back where they came from. Ali's story gave me a wider awareness and prevented me from these cold-hearted views. Ali has been given a chance to be Australia, though he is still struggling to hold on to that hope. Ali was told he was to stay in the detention centre in Curtin, WA for forty-five days, at which time he would receive a permanent visa.

'After all that time, the forty-five days, they said the law has been changed and now they get a visa that is called a temporary protection visa, which is for three years. People stayed longer in detention without knowing what is happening to their cases. Are they being processed or are they just on the shelves? So I had to stay there about five months and a half.'

Two years since arriving in Australia, Ali lives alone on allowances from the government. He was given a six-month course in English, and has learnt to balance a life of study with a life of paying for electricity, phone, water bills and rent – all things that someone his age rarely has to deal with. Looking at Ali I see a man, now twenty years of age, who had been living in Australia for the past two years and at heart is an Australian. I find it ironic that those in our community with the most extraordinary stories and the most to teach us about our ignorance in matters of concern in the world are the ones who struggle to find acceptance here. This aside, Ali is extremely grateful for the chances Australia has given him, and in turn I am extremely grateful for Ali and the way he has opened my eyes.

Blackbirding: The Loss of an Idyllic Lifestyle

by Tshala Jenkins, aged 12

Blackbirding is what my great grandparents, Corowa and Iahipe, went through. Corowa and Iahipe were their last names but in Australia they were given another name, like Jacob Iahipe and John Corowa. And sometime later Iahipe was changed to Ivey. They were given these names because they were easier to say than their islander names.

Corowa and Iahipe were made slaves in Australia but before this they were happily living in Tanna, an island in the Melanesian group of islands. They were native tribal men with their own lores and customs (this is the way to spell laws in Vanuatu). They were looking forward to becoming elders in their own village and island.

Around the 1860s or 1900s Corowa and Iahipe were tricked and bribed about working in Australia on the cane fields in Brisbane with a three year contract. The way they were tricked was this: because they couldn't speak English they used hand signals. When the Europeans arrived to pick up the slaves they held up three fingers. My great grandparents and other men took it as meaning three months. The Europeans knew they meant three years and they purposely tricked them.

They didn't know they were being tricked and bribed. They were lured onto the 'slave train', a huge sailing boat that went from island to island picking up slaves when they were young men.

When they arrived in Australia life was very harsh, as they had to work for their own food. Some didn't even get food at all because of the white Australia policy.

They lived like natives but they were slowly losing their customs because of the Europeans who had claimed the land from the original natives; and the Europeans imposed their own laws.

They then rode south by horseback to the Tweed Heads/ Brunswick Heads area because the farmers there offered better conditions than those they experienced on the cane fields in Queensland.

Because they were there for three years, they had settled down and made a family. Jacob Iahipe married a woman from the Bundjalung people of the Tweed Byron area and John Corowa married an Aboriginal woman from the same region.

As the Europeans spread they cleared cedar from the mountains and they wiped out the rainforests. They had nothing left, so the natives went to missions.

So, thanks to European colonisation, we now have super-markets and no more bush tucker.

From a Small Detention Centre, I am Now in a Bigger Detention Centre: The Story of an Afghan Refugee

by Zac Darab, aged 14

What is a refugee? The abstract nature of their representation through the Australian media denies the essential individuality of these people. Refugees are repeatedly presented as a category of undesirable people. They are portrayed in such a way as to incite moral panic in the community – often for political purposes. For instance, frequently it is implied that they are terrorists, smugglers of weapons, drugs or carriers of disease. Perhaps the defining example of this was the Tampa incident, and associated events during which it was alleged that refugees were throwing their children overboard.

Who could forget the Australian government suggesting that these people were somehow lesser human beings than those we would welcome in Australia? Although the allegations were eventually revealed as a political stunt, the impoverished view of refugees was not corrected. In light of this, I saw it as being very important to put a human face to at least one of these displaced people and have him inform others of his story and experiences about being a refugee.

After hearing Riz Wakil speak at a public meeting on Australian refugee policy, I was so moved that I wanted other Australians to hear what it means to be a refugee in Australia in 2002. Riz is a refugee who comes from the province of Hazara in central Afghanistan. He currently resides in Sydney. When I contacted Riz about interviewing him, he was delighted to be chosen and have the opportunity to explain his situation.

I feel humbled and honoured to have met Riz Wakil. At only twenty-two years of age, he had endured such incredible hardship and, at the time of the interview, he continued to be under pressure from the Immigration department. Despite his personal turmoil, he welcomed me into his home and treated me to his hospitality.

Riz's story of becoming an asylum seeker began when he was eighteen years of age. He said: 'Unfortunately in Afghanistan we are born in a war-torn country. We had no opportunity to go to school and get even basic education. It was an official sentence from the authorities in Afghanistan that Hazara people are not allowed to study.'

Riz went on to explain that the Hazara people had been oppressed long before the Taliban took control. 'We, the Hazara, are the third minority group and we have been badly treated for centuries.' His community was excluded from the social goods like education and access to medical resources, Riz said, because they were not of the highest socio-economic status, and they were seen as inferior to the ruling party, the Pashtu.

Riz was forced to leave his country and his family to try and find a better quality of life elsewhere. His journey, however, was not easy. 'We didn't have any proper documentation because the country was destroyed and there was no one to supply us with proper documentation, so it was illegal to leave Afghanistan. When we left Afghanistan, I spent a few weeks in Pakistan just to get the proper travel document and after that I came to Indonesia. Everything was arranged and after that I spent about six weeks in Indonesia before catching the boat.'

He did not have the luxury of coming to Australia by plane, instead he came by a 'leaky boat'. 'There was seventy-three people on that tiny little fishing boat, sixty Afghans and thirteen Iraqi refugees including two kids and one family.' Shoulder-to-shoulder, no facilities, no room to stretch or to lie down, no privacy for personal ablutions and the constant fear of being swamped in the rising swell. Nor did the fear subside when they reached Australian waters. 'They didn't allow us to land on Ashmore Reef Island. They kept us on the boat. After two days navy officials came out. We said, "We are sick and we are having medical problems, you should help us." The only answer we get from the officer, he said, "Next time try to catch a plane. Don't come by boat." He didn't have any sympathy for the people. It took them another two days to bring us from Ashmore Reef Island to Broome.'

This is the greeting that Riz received when he arrived in Australia. Coming from a land-locked country, it was only recently that Riz and most of the passengers had actually seen the ocean, let alone sailed across it in a tiny vessel. They were traumatised from their journey. For all the refugees who had fled their countries because they were so poorly treated, it must not have felt so different when they arrived in Australia. In Broome, Riz was told that his application would be processed within forty-five days. He was then escorted to Curtin Detention Centre where he received a basic health check and was searched to ensure that he was not bringing anything illegal into the country. Riz was then taken into detention where he remained for nine months.

Curtin Detention Centre used to be an airforce base but has since been converted into a detention centre. After his extended period of incarceration, Riz was ecstatic to hear that he was allowed into the community. He was issued with a temporary visa, which is valid for thirty-six months. The sense of freedom he experienced when learning of his release faded somewhat when Riz learned what a temporary visa meant for him.

'I found out that from a small detention centre, I am now in bigger detention centre. I cannot meet one of my family members. I cannot go out of Australia if I ever want to re-enter. It doesn't matter if anything happens to your family back there, I cannot go and visit. For me this is an imprisonment as well.'

On a temporary visa, Riz cannot move forward, nor can he go back. He cannot return to Afghanistan because his life was so poor over there and the country is now at war. Nor can he move forward and establish his life in Australia because with a temporary status, his future is very hazy. Also he feels incredibly sad about the hardship his family is experiencing. Riz said, 'My family members are desperate to get out of Afghanistan but I am not allowed to sponsor them and I am not allowed to bring them here.' On a brighter note, however, Riz is allowed to work, and he says that 'definitely, the majority of refugees on protection visas, they are working'.

Another major concern for Riz was that he could not study in Australia. Under the conditions of a temporary visa, in order to study he would have to pay international student fees. 'One of my friends, he is paying I think $18,000 per annum for a basic computer course and now because his visa is going to expire, he cannot concentrate on his study.' For Riz this is a no win situation. He is excluded from the benefits that Australians take for granted. Riz explains that he can understand why he did not get an education in Afghanistan, but now in Australia because of the government policy concerning temporary protection visas, once again he is not allowed to study.

Riz recounted that before September 11, 2001, it was possible to apply for a permanent residence in Australia. However, after this date the laws regarding visas changed. His visa is now forever temporary and he cannot apply for permanent protection. Riz said, 'The Immigration department says very, very clear in that letter that we have to come and convince Immigration department because Immigration thinks that in Afghanistan everything is all right. It is all right for refugees to go even though it's not safe for Australian tourists to go.'

Is Riz's life less valuable than the life of an Australian citizen?

Riz is a productive member of the Australian community. He is currently working in a printing company. He is paying taxes, paying rent, consuming goods and services, and generally contributing to the Australian economy. 'In free time, I am working with the refugee organisations to do something for the people inside detention centres, and to help people who are desperate to go to another country; and for those already in the community on a temporary visa.' Even under threat of deportation, Riz is generous in giving his time to help others. He is industrious, law-abiding and community-minded, as well as being keen to learn and to acquire new skills.

If Riz is forced to return to Afghanistan, he will face persecution. He stated,

'When we were there our struggle was not only to get rid of Taliban, our struggle was for a secular society which gives all the minorities, the religious minorities, the ethnic minorities, the proper representation and proper rights in Afghanistan. And this is a threat for the Islamic fundamentalist government. So that's why I think for us even they have not destroyed Taliban yet. I don't believe they have destroyed Taliban. They are underground and they are working. As we see in the news that there are attacks even on the President. There are attacks on the US forces, on the civilian properties and civilian people.'

If Riz stays in Australia it is quite likely that he will also face racist attitudes here. He believes that people have nothing personal against him but the government has put out so much propaganda against refugees. He believes that the government's current policies are racist and extremely detrimental to him and people in similar positions.

'And now I think while I am in Australia, I didn't achieve anything. I had fear for my life in Afghanistan and I have fear for my life in Australia as well. I don't know what will happen after thirty months. So I cannot do anything. Still I am afraid what will happen. The other thing, we have been targeted by the ethnic majorities and we have been targeted by racism here. When we go outside and introduce ourselves as Afghans, all the people here, because of the propaganda, they think all the people from the Middle East, they are terrorists and they are harmful for the society.'

You now know Riz Wakil's story. At the age of twenty-two, he has experienced intense disadvantage, which is unimaginable to me and to most Australians. He has been persecuted, faced heavy seas in a tiny fishing boat, been incarcerated and conferred a temporary status in a country renowned for giving people a 'fair go'. Despite all this, Riz continues to strive for freedom but his visa is now limited to four months. He has proved himself to be hard working in improving his job skills, perfecting his English and spending his time helping other refugees. Riz would be an asset to our country. I would appeal to the Australian people to lobby for Riz and other refugees who have fled war-torn countries. In the war against terrorism, Riz is a victim and he needs our support.

AND A TEAR MIGHT COME TO MY EYE

'My friend and I collected her favourite flower
and placed it where she lay asleep before
the bomb.'

Untitled

by Nooria Wazefadost, aged 15

Since I opened my eyes into this world I heard the sound of rockets, missiles and all kinds of artillery firing around my house. Thousands of other Afghan infants and children were mourning all around my country. All mothers were screaming and shouting next to the dead bodies of children. All of my mind is filled with fearful sounds of weapons and portraits of barbarous people's faces and visions of acts and cruelty in front of my eyes.

I don't have any good memory of my childhood. One of my memories is that of losing my playmates. One day my friend named Maryam was sleeping next to her mother, and was suddenly blown in the air by an explosion from a Soviet Union bomb. Her body was never found. My friend Fatimeh and I collected her favourite flower and placed it where she lay asleep before the bomb.

One of my heart-rending memories is about my friend Zahra. After several months when I was about eleven and a half years old, I heard that Zahra died in Pakistan and her story, as I know it, began five years ago like this . . .

I didn't know her very well, she was in our school, but in different classes because she was four years older than me. I could easily understand and feel, from her situation and the way she was clothed, that their family was poor. I could understand from her beautiful and lovely smile that she was soft-natured, kind and delicate.

One year passed and our friendship developed. I was interested in her special behaviour and ability.

One day the land of Bamian, where I was living, suddenly changed. The selfish, disobedient and above itself Taliban arrived near the gates of the compact and crowded city. The people of the city were scared and they were praying that they might get out of the city but that didn't happen. The once gay and bustling streets of the city became quiet and boring.

On a summer morning I woke up, I felt awful and I didn't know what was happening, I told my mum that I didn't feel like going to school. She didn't respond to me for a long time. But I think she tried desperately to hide her agitation but her tears couldn't stop. Then she told me, 'no one is going to school today.' I didn't ask her for any explanation because I understood that the groups of Taliban had come to the city. The schools, like other places in Bamian, were ruined and destroyed. But I hadn't any news from Zahra and other friends. The time was passing slowly, I was sad and miserable. I missed my school, teachers and friends.

One day, without my mother's permission, I ran to Zahra's house. I knocked on the door. Zahra opened the door, everything was too quiet. She didn't tell me anything for two or three minutes. Then her tears streamed from her motionless eyes to her dry lips. Her mother was crying and shrieked in pain, 'They killed Ali.' Ali was Zahra's father and was working in the energy factory. When I heard that, suddenly my books fall from my hands. I couldn't believe it.

I came back home. When mother saw that my face was red and asked me what happened, the only thing I could say was, 'Zahra's father has been killed.' My mum knew what was going on in my heart and didn't ask me any more and tears were running from her eyes.

My mum and I went to Zahra's house. Poor Zahra hadn't any older or younger brother, only twin sisters younger than her. Her mother had been sick for two or three years. Zahra had to take the responsibility for her two young sisters and her sick mother. She had to work and bring some food for them and pay the rent for the house. Even in that time the women hadn't the right to work outside. What choice did they have?

Days, weeks, months passed and the people of my city were moving the dead bodies of their beloved to the place where before there was a park. The park of the city had become a cemetery. Zahra and her family migrated to Pakistan and they resided in Peshawar. Then she married an Afghan man called Mohammed from Hazareh ethnic group (which is mine and Zahra's group). After her marriage, her mother died because of her sickness. And the twin sisters were left alone at home and blown off by the bomb. She was left alone in this horrible world, living alone and isolated in an unknown city. For Zahra, life was lonely, dull and helpless.

Mohammed, her husband, went to Europe. After he left, she lived with the darkness of the situation. A few days later she got a letter from her husband:

Dear Zahra

Hope u okay and after a few minutes we'll go to the boat and I hope to get the visa and bring you here to start a new life, I love you and take care until that day.

One day the neighbours came and told Zahra that someone phoned her, she thought that it is her husband. She got so happy and start to run. But when she picked up the phone it was Mohammed's sister, who told her that Mohammed had drowned in the middle of a stormy ocean. The phone fell from her hand.

She returned home and didn't come out for two days and no one had any news from her. On the third day the owner of the house came and knocked on the door many times but no one opened the door, then he opened the door with his own key.

Zahra wasn't in the home. There was silence and quiet. The door of the bathroom was closed. He opened the door. Zahra had killed herself and ended her depressing life.

Police arrived and looked around to find out why she killed herself. They found a note in her album, which had the photos of her father, mother, twin sisters and her husband in it. In the note was her writing:

Don't judge me, I wasn't weak; I was the only candle in my family which was burning through this life. I endured the death of each person in my family and after my last hope was extinguished. I had two choices. One, Die; and the second one was put arrogance aside, which was the worst thing in my life! I choose the first one. I wanted to die in Afghanistan but . . .

This was the story of my friend, which will remain with me forever.

During this time I was still going to school and the only thing I wanted was to finish my education, but very soon the Taliban closed the school which girls used to attend.

My people or Hazareh people were discriminated against, and the Taliban raped the Hazareh women, hung men, children were kidnapped and houses were destroyed. In this situation there was no opportunity and safety, so my parents decided to migrate somewhere else, but didn't know where! One day we set off on our journey to a peaceful land or country. It was the year 2002. After journeying from Afghanistan to Pakistan, the hot weather without transport was really hard. Especially for my mum, because she was pregnant.

In Pakistan the smuggler took all of our money and told us to go to Australia. He said, Australia is an 'Eden' and defends always human rights. He sent us to Indonesia, where my mum gave birth to a little son. She had an operation and it was so difficult for her.

After ten days, we moved to the small boat. It was a very dangerous and exciting journey. We hadn't ever seen a boat and the ocean. I had to be strong for my little sisters, brothers, father and mother because I was the oldest child. A few days later we were sailing on the water of the Pacific and Indian Ocean. It was terrifying and horrible for all of us, mainly when the boat was sailing in the storms. Hundreds of times we thought we would drown in the darkness of the ocean, the horrible and haunting sounds of the water which wanted to swallow us.

After ten days out at sea our boat was guided by an Australian naval ship. Finally, we arrived in Australia. I can't picture the most joyful and happiest memories of the day we arrived on Australian land. I thought my miserable life was over and new horizons of life with its fortunes and happiness would welcome us. But my dream was not realised. I found myself including my family and other refugees in a detention centre, gaoled, faced with fences all around.

After hearing a lot of excellent things about Australia, for me it was unbelievable, that the same country had placed us in a detention centre.

We stayed in a detention centre for two months and the situation in there was terrible, everyone worried about the future and the hot weather was uncomfortable.

After our stay at the centre we were given a temporary protection visa (TPV) for three years which cuts my future prospects. I'm a refugee, that's why I can understand the refugee's hardship and difficulties.

Now I am in Sydney. I spent nine months in an Intensive English Centre (IEC). I am planning for my future to study hard and become a doctor. I'm doing year ten at the moment. And the students and teachers are lovely. I like Australia so much and I don't want to go back to my country and I can prove that it is not safe. I hope to stay in Australia forever.

The Place Where God Died

by Melanie Poole, aged 18

Preface

At Auschwitz, tell me, where was God?
The answer – Where was Man?

When Jostein Gaarder, author of *Sophie's World*, wrote these words, he conveyed a very important message: that 'God', being the symbol of love, compassion and benevolence cannot be present where barbarism, persecution and injustice prevail. He saw 'God' as a spirit present only in humanity, manifested in acts of love and kindness. When Gaarder heard the stories of the detainees in the Auschwitz concentration camp of World War II, and the horrific cruelty they had been subjected to, he was convinced that, in such circumstances, any notion of 'God' is destroyed.

Gyzele Osmani is a refugee who tells a story of persecution and cruelty, of the unnecessary suffering of the innocent, of places where the qualities represented by 'God' cease to exist. Most particularly, Gyzele's story reveals truths that many do not want to believe, truths about what happens to refugees in the 'lucky country'; truths that will inevitably leave the reader asking themselves what has happened to humanity.

Fleeing from Persecution

In 1999, Serbian soldiers marched into East Kosovo and forced Kosovo Albanian villagers out of their homes at gunpoint. Gyzele Osmani, then a twenty-nine year old Kosovo Albanian mother of five, was washing clothes when the soldiers arrived and told her to vacate her home within ten minutes. Terrified, she called her husband and children (aged nineteen months to six years) together, and the family fled, leaving behind everything they owned.

'There was fire and gunshots and shouting . . . there were bodies on the streets . . . They were . . . raping the women and there were screams and agonising cries coming from everywhere . . . We ran and ran until it was left behind.'

The family walked for six hours before reaching the house of friends who lived in Macedonia. They stayed with these friends for two nights, after which they again walked for hours to catch a bus that would take them to a refugee camp. They spent over eighteen hours waiting for the bus, during which time there was no food and nothing but water to give the children.

When they reached the camp, four of the five children had developed illnesses and Gyzele's youngest daughter (one of her nineteen month old twins) was found to have a dislocated hip, thought to be a result of the long journey and the hours she had spent with her legs at unnatural angles while on her mother's hip.

A doctor examined the baby and told Gyzele that, unless she was operated upon, she would never walk properly. He then advised Gyzele to apply to be taken to either Australia, Canada or America. Gyzele applied for all three, desperate to find somewhere with adequate conditions for her children. Within several weeks, she was told she would receive temporary protection in Australia, something that filled her with overwhelming joy and relief.

'I thought to myself, "Now my children will have place that is safe with many opportunities for the future." My husband and I were so happy. We thought "Australian people are so kind".'

On 15th July 1999, Gyzele and her family arrived by plane in Sydney, Australia. They stayed in Sydney for five days and then were taken to the Bandiana Safe Haven in Albury Wodonga. Here they met with support workers who made them feel safe and welcome and arranged for medical care for the children.

Gyzele's daughter underwent three operations over ten months, however all were unsuccessful. She was booked in for a fourth operation when suddenly the news came that the government had decided it was time for the family to be deported.

'It was war in my country. They said that it was safe now in Kosovo because the United Nations were there and we could all go back. But we did not think it would be safe in East Kosovo. There were no United Nations there, not in our village. We had no place to go. If we went back we would be in a tent, we would have nothing. We were scared to go back.'

The government refused to listen, however, and the Osmanis were told that if they did not leave Australia they would be detained. Gyzele did not know what detention was, but did not think it could be worse than what her family would be forced to endure if they returned to East Kosovo.

'I thought; "The Australian people are kind. It is good here. Nothing can be as bad as in my country." Also, staying here was the only chance my daughter had of being able to walk again.'

So the Osmani family stayed in Australia, despite the severe threats and fear tactics the Department of Immigration and Multicultural and Indigenous Affairs (DIMIA) officers used to try to convince them to leave.

'They told us that in detention everybody would hate us and try to hurt us. They say we will regret it if we do not leave. But we still think that maybe Immigration will change their mind and let us stay to live.'

Seven Months in Hell

Immediately after Gyzele and her family made it clear to Immigration that they were too afraid to return to their country, they were arrested and taken to the Port Hedland Detention Centre in Western Australia. The sight that greeted them was beyond any Gyzele had comprehended.

'It was horrible. All desert . . . No trees, no flowers. My children kept asking "Where are we? Where are the flowers?" I could tell them nothing. They kept saying "We want to go. Please we go away from here." They kept crying and crying . . . It was a very, very bad place.'

Gyzele and her family lived in a building with 200 other people. Conditions were terrible, with poor facilities and little space. As a result, disease was rife and within days Gyzele's entire family fell ill. As the detention centre was run by Australian Correctional Management (ACM), a private company, everything was done at minimum cost. The meals were meagre portions of partially cooked rice, with occasional serves of basic fruits and vegetables. To wash with, detainees were issued with bottles of chemicals labelled 'shampoo' which burned Gyzele's children's scalps, and caused their hair to become brittle and dry.

The 'education' program was held in a crowded room and taught by poorly paid, under resourced teachers. It was also selective; only 'good' children who didn't protest or cry or ask for extra food when they were hungry were allowed to be educated. There were also many times when Gyzele's children were not allowed to receive education because there was not enough room or paper and pencils for them.

Within the detention centre there were 400 children and, of all the abhorrent things she witnessed, Gyzele found the most heartbreaking to be seeing them deprived of nutrition, medical care, education and, most significantly, their freedom.

'How can they lock up children? How can they lock up any innocent people, but especially how can they lock up children?'

There were numerous stories of the suffering other detainees had endured whilst in detention, stories that Gyzele will never forget. One particular woman from China had been detained for five years and seven months. During her first month she had given birth and so her five and a half year old had grown up incarcerated, never having tasted freedom at all. Her other child, who was two years old when they arrived in Australia, could not remember anything but his time in detention. Gyzele said she would never forget those two children, who suffered from depression despite their young ages, and who seldom laughed or smiled.

'The children there weren't like children I'd seen before . . . Many of them had no hope . . . Many wanted to die.'

A constant battle that Gyzele fought while in detention was for her daughter to be re-operated on, as she was still unable to walk properly and suffered frequent pain. When Gyzele finally was allowed to see a doctor, he x-rayed her daughter and Gyzele, who had no medical knowledge, could see that it was quite clear that her hip was out of place. Before the doctor could talk to her, however, Gyzele was escorted out of the room while ACM guards spoke to him.

When Gyzele re-entered the doctor's office, she was not allowed to speak to him without the ACM guards present. The doctor – a spinal and orthopaedic specialist, turned to Gyzele and said, rather nervously,

'I'm afraid I don't know anything about this. I can't help you.'

Gyzele could tell that the doctor was unable to speak the truth in front of the guards and so she decided she would ring him. When she requested the doctor's phone number, however, she was not allowed to have it. Gyzele's daughter still cannot walk properly.

'The ACM scared everybody. They gave threats to all the kind people, all our friends. There were some nice ACM, like one woman who hug me once. She was in a lot of trouble, they say to her, "You are not allowed to hug these people. You cannot talk to them unless they ask you questions or you are giving orders. You must refer to them only by number, not by name." '

Gyzele recalls being told that if she asked for extra food, or talked to the media, or protested, then the government would 'blacklist' her and she would never live in Australia. Consequently most detainees were too scared to speak out though some, having reached a point of utter desperation, tried to protest against their treatment.

After seven months in detention, Marion Lé, a well-known human rights lawyer, came to the aid of the Osmani family and secured permanent residence in Australia for them. Such was the Osmanis' gratitude that they decided to move to Canberra simply to be near Marion.

Epilogue

Since being released from detention, Gyzele has actively campaigned for refugee rights. She attends protest marches, writes letters to MPs and, perhaps most importantly, continues to share her experiences. 'It is only through revealing truth,' says Gyzele, 'that anything will ever be changed.'

Gyzele's children still suffer nightmares and have found adjusting to 'normal' life very difficult. 'In Port Hedland the guards came into our rooms at night, waking everybody to see our identification tags. They would flash their torches and yell our numbers, as though we were dogs. I used to say, "My children are not going to run away, please let them sleep." Now the children wake up in the night screaming, thinking that the guards are by their beds.'

Gyzele has not lost faith in the Australian people, however, and frequently mentions the kindness of people like Marion Lé. 'I think the Australian people are mostly very kind. But I can never forgive the Australian Government. I cannot forgive the nightmares and the trauma and the suffering. Not the lies and the threats and the cruelty. No, never can I forgive that.'

If Jostein Gaarder were to hear the story of Gyzele Osmani, I think he would surely ask himself where – in all the talk of 'legislative framework' and 'tough border control' and 'profit margins' and 'parliamentary debate' – is humanity?

I think he would wonder what happened to those wonderful rights enshrined by the United Nations in the Universal Declaration of Human Rights and The Rights of the Child, such as everyone having the right to liberty, education and freedom of speech, and being innocent until proven guilty.

Like most of us, he would probably wonder 'why'; and, like most of us, would probably find no answer.

> '. . . *This is the place that will inhabit you*
> *This is the place you cannot imagine*
> *This is the place that will finally defeat you*
> *Where the word why shrivels*
> *And empties itself.'*

– Margaret Atwood 'Notes Toward A Poem That Can Never Be Written.'*

---

*© Margaret Atwood. Used by permission of the author.

A Refugee

by Mohammad Zia, aged 18

Born in a country that is totally devastated in decades of a war that has left no sign of justice, humanity and freedom. Especially for people like me who were born into a minority ethnic group to be the victim of discrimination and slavery of the majority ethnic groups. Pushed away from most of the major cities and our property towards the harshest part of the country because of being in a minority without enough power to defend our rights.

Free but you can't move, stuck in one particular part of the country, cut off from the rest of the world. The majority ethnic group surrounds all around this land without access to any sort of facility, from food, market, business transportation etc. We can't claim our rights for fear of facing sanctions or fear they will stop the flow of food and people would die as a result of starvation. So struggling for our life away from the sight of the world trying not to be ashamed of who we are which has been the case for decades.

The nineties, when a new foreign regime took over the country from a neighbouring country, were the worst for the minority ethnic groups, because the majority ethnic group was in favour of the new regime. They took advantage of the power as much they could and started their full retaliation on the minority ethnic group who were claiming their basic rights. So they cleared their way and made every single person obey whatever they wanted and no one would be able to claim their rights in the country except them. Because it is more than a century that we had been trying not to be the victim of brutality, slavery and patronisation.

They took over to carry out their deadly plan and massacred thousands of people from children to oldest people, even animals, to pull off the root and sign of minority ethnic group. As a fifteen-year-old, that was the darkest moment of my life to see the bodies of hundreds of people who were executed and children the same as my age and younger were hanging on the power poles in a cruel way. My heart was bleeding to see the cruelty of human beings towards human beings and my feeling was melting away my body from head to toe. The feeling of brutality of humans – it's that I would never be able to explain in words.

My childhood is stolen and I can't remember one good day with other children except being always on high alert of security, occupation and death. On top of that they started sending the entire young male population to the front line of war against our own people to conquer the rest of the country. So most of the people gave up their hope and started to send their young and unexperienced kids out of the country to the next neighbouring country in hope of shelter in other humanitarian countries of the world.

Our exhausted country was really stuffed by the new regime. Any sort of media was banned. All the schools, universities, any sort of education systems were destroyed, closed down or became their military base. A few schools were left open to cover up their shit but they changed subjects to religious stuff and no sign of science and technology and development as before. That was the only way for them to run their government and their business. To keep people in darkness and cut them off from the rest of the world. It became a world of men and women not allowed to work, study or do any other activity as before. They were not even allowed to go to the doctor. Which means if you are sick, bad luck, die at home or recover automatically without a second chance.

As I mentioned before people were trying to get out. But leaving of the country wasn't that easy and it was 90 per cent death. Because of the instability and brutality of the majority ethnic group that had been controlling the country, they divided the country between their tribal leaders. So everything from government to transport was under their control. The only way to get out was through the enemies' smugglers. We knew that those smugglers take people and search them in the middle of the way to take their money off them then dump them in a mass grave, which was their routine job. But we had to trust them because we had no options left.

So after a few months living in hiding with my mum she decided to send me out of the country in fear that I would be sent in the frontline of war. Dad was in custody in the south of the country and was due to be released after six months. He was accused of running a business in the majority control area. As I said, being in the minority, we were not allowed to go out of that particular surrounded block of land and work in other parts of the country.

On that morning I left my homeland as a fifteen-year-old, tossed up my life to travel in the heart of the majority ethnic group by smuggler, to pass to the neighbouring country without previous experience with more chance of death, which was not easy for me but a nightmare for my family.

The sky was full of black clouds and foggy and was not in a good mood, which was looking frightening. The people around me in a small dirty bus were looking suspicious and they kept staring at me. As I was looking outside through the coach's window the environment was dead, devastated, harsh, dirty and nasty. The environment that swallowed thousands and millions of human beings. I couldn't see anything except devastation.

The weather was so dusty that the distance a few metres away was invisible because of the dust like powder coming out from under the wheels of the vehicles and running in the air higher than the height of the vehicles. Which was really showing the nature of the devastation and isolation of the human beings.

Even the vehicles couldn't dare chase each other or overtake because of the devastated rough surface of the road. Everything was looking exhausted, devastated, in tears, quiet, sad and was it seems complaining from human's behaviour. I couldn't even hear the sound of bomb and grenade blast, which was a familiar sound that I had grown up with, nor the passengers that were talking around me.

I was not looking to people because I didn't want to see hundreds of eyes full of blood staring at me. Outside was full of pieces of technology from computers, TVs, tape cassettes and research equipment and hospital's stuff that was hanging on every power pole. As I said their ridiculous religious dogma was to disgrace or tint our nation's religion, history, custom and push people back to 15th century. As I was in a world of dreams I had a feeling that someone was trying to talk to me and I couldn't hear, my body was so exhausted that I couldn't respond to my feeling. I tried to talk but I wasn't able so I ignored and remained as I was. It was like I had no connection with my body. So once I felt pain on my face and I was like woken up, I found a man standing opposite me and laughing at me. I looked at my body to see anything unusual that he was laughing at. All I could see was my top covered in blood and the man swearing and humiliating me in front of everyone in the coach. Everyone was laughing and no one was there with a sense of humanity to be on my side and protect me.

I was gazing around in the bus and seeking help from someone. The wicked man remained standing in front of me and asked me in abusive language to leave the coach. I was totally patronised, dehumanised, humiliated and knocked out of the coach that I had already paid double fare for and no one said why except teasing me. It was night time, a dark night in autumn, in freezing conditions – it was down to minus 40 in some parts. All I can remember when touching any sort of metal or piece of steel my hands getting stuck and I couldn't take my hands off the metal. My hands' skin was out of clothes frozen and started to break up.

It was a frightening and humiliating night. A night in a world of loneliness, a night of total injustice, first night that I was without my family, a night with no one to console me and a night of brutality on the middle of nowhere. A night without a moon and I couldn't even see the stars properly, just hundreds of vehicles running in every direction. I was on the side of the road and every motorist was laughing at me, which was like something slicing every single part of my weakened body.

After passing the darkest night of my life in that freezing condition I didn't expect to survive but I did survive to bear the rest of the harshness of life that came only on top of us and we have to bear. Anyway in the early morning while my body was half frozen and I had given up the hope of life, I managed to stand up on the road in the way of a truck to die under its wheels or to get on board. Finally the truck stopped, and through pleading and paying some money, the driver agreed not to squash me in a spot under the load of his truck like piece of rubbish. He agreed to keep me away from the sight of other people for three days without food and little bit of water that I had with me. Finally I arrived in the neighbouring country not fully dead and not fully alive.

In Pakistan with a world of uncertainty without documents or understanding the language. In a strange country I didn't know where to go or what to do in fear of getting caught by police. In country that had a history of human rights violation and an unbalanced society. On the other hand scared that I could see the new regime that was in my country because Pakistan was their main homeland to get training and support and cross the border to create devastation in my homeland. So there was no doubt that I could be caught in Pakistan as well. Anyway I hung around for the whole day although I hadn't eaten for three days and my stomach was squashed, but because of the language problem I was not even able to buy some food while I couldn't stand up.

After a while a couple got my attention and they were speaking the language of a tiny ethnic group in my country. Although I didn't know that language properly, at least I was able to solve my problem because that language was a part of my school study for a while. When I approached them and started to talk to them and they looked at my pale face and my situation, they said come with us tonight because now it's too late and we will be able to help you tomorrow. I went to their temporary and small boarding house to spend the night there, then I found we were the same nationality but they came from some European country for a family reunion. I spent that night full of messy dreams and the next morning the two nice couples introduced me to smugglers who had a staff that could speak my language to help me to get somewhere.

The smugglers asked me to pay $6000 – it will cover all your expenses, accommodation, false documents, flight to Indonesia then the ship fare to Australia, one of the humanitarian countries that can help you. But not your other expenses once you are out of Pakistan. I was so worried that they might leave me behind like those people in the bus. Anyway I had to trust and I paid the money that my mother gave. I was so lucky that I was not searched while travelling in my own country. But after paying their money nothing was left for me except a few hundred. The money that I had I have no idea how my mum managed it. Sold her jewellery, borrowed, sold something from the house, gave all they had, nothing left for them. God knows and I still have absolutely no idea.

So they accommodated me in a small dirty flat with two others that I didn't know and I couldn't even speak their language. Waiting for nothing and I had no hope because no one was trustable in that part of the world and everyone is like a hunter to get money and run away. For two weeks stuck in room for no hope, while my body was exhausted of humiliation and dehumanisation. I was not allowed to go out because I would get caught.

After a few weeks they managed to make false documents to send me to Indonesia. Some people were deported from the airport because of false passports. Finally I passed the check-in and our flight was ready to go. After a few transits in other countries we arrived in Indonesia. Someone from smugglers' network picked me up and took me to a motel. In Indonesia the situation was not good because the police were catching people every day. After a few days the smugglers began sending people to Australia. But we had to travel about three and half days by bus to the nearest island of Indonesia to get to Australia. The next morning we started to go island to island with uncertain future to be able to catch a so-called ship. We were going with our bus into ship carrier to jump island to island. After travelling three days in the coach I was tired and hungry. I was trying to eat some food that was supplied by the bus but I couldn't eat that leftover food.

Anyway after seventy-five hours squashed in the coach we were about to arrive at the island that they were talking about. We received a phone call from the first bus that had departed ten hours before our bus that Indonesian police had caught them and were looking for us in other parts of the island as well. So we had to turn and go back seventy-five hours to Bali where we came from. Everyone was tired, sick and quiet, didn't have the energy for argument. We came seventy-five hours back to Bali. One week squashed in a bus that never had a stop or break to stretch our body except for fuel. Every one became sick because being one week in the bus and eating the leftover food and then for one week we were all in hotels or motels and taking basic medication to recover.

After about ten days when everyone had recovered from the week before and the arrested people came back, the smugglers began their second attempt to send us. But this time we succeeded to reach the island and I could see a small boat far away in ocean and each time a few people were going in her by another little boat. We were half of us in the boat and I was with the other half on the beach when the police again caught us.

But this time it was the whole group of us and we were kept for the whole night in freezing conditions but in the morning the people who had a visa were sent back to Bali and the people with expired visas were taken away. Back to our first location, stressed and given up any sort of hope for success and everyone was blaming the smugglers and for most us our one month visa had expired. But a few days later the third attempt started but this time they paid huge amounts of money to Indonesian coast guard to send us away without any doubt because their cost for the first two attempt had blown up in the air. So we started to come to Australia.

Yet again tossing up our lives in the endless ocean to Australia, 150 cramped up in a small and leaky Indonesian fishing boat that we had been told was a big luxury ship! It was my first journey that I ever had on the ocean and in a boat that had nothing except a small engine and a broken frame. Everyone around me was exhausted, depressed, no one had the energy for even talking to each other. Because of exhaustion and most of them young and inexperienced no one had checked whether there was enough food or water. A few hours later we found out that there was not sufficient food and water for us in a journey that we didn't know how long it would take.

But we managed to supply only one meal and one small bottle of water per person per day. The mechanics that we had on board were working tirelessly around the clock on the engine of the boat to keep it running. Because the boat was small with too many people on board the engine was exhausted. Other people were on different shifts to throw water with buckets out of that leaky boat.

Travelling in a world of uncertainty sacrificed by the brutality of human beings. Every where was water, without any island around. The sun was rising from one side of the ocean and setting on the other side of the ocean.

Mostly at night we were facing storms and high waves. The storm and waves were throwing our boat like a piece of rubbish weightless everywhere and water passing from the top of us and making everyone wet. More chance to be drowned. After seven days our lives got threatening because we had run out of food and water.

A Story of a Life

by Nitya Devi Dambiec, aged 16

This is the story of Albana Derguti, a year ten student and refugee who fled war in Kosovo, Albania.

When I asked about Albania, I was told of many things. There was a river that gave hot water, bubbling out from a rock. There were concerts and singing, school and soccer: 'We played soccer every day nearly . . . in Europe everybody is crazy about soccer.' I was told of a grandfather's farm: 'I loved it . . . there were lots of animals, and they were beautiful.' At night the streetlights would come on and the teenagers would gather outside, talking and roller-blading down the steepest hills.

There are good memories, but the world is not perfect and nor was Albania. In learning of a river that gives hot water and a farm of beautiful animals, I was also told of the persecution of Albanians by the Serbian government. 'I love European history and the story of my country is good to tell, but Albanians were persecuted, everything was more difficult for you if you were Albanian.' Albanians could not work in the government, police force or other areas of the public service. The men were dis-liked most of all. People react to situations which they do not like and, inevitably, the men of Albania grew up. As told by Albana: 'The war started because Albanians made up an army to fight the Serbians.' Soldiers were everywhere, the lights went off and they were not able to go outside. Everything was so close by and one could hear the gunshots even when inside. This was not a place to live and to learn and to grow up with a family: 'We wanted to run away from the war, we didn't want to stay there.'

I knew already the next part of the story. I knew that Albana had left the sounds and sights of the fighting, because we now sat on the grass in the sun. She told me of her departure from Albania. They caught a train to Macedonia. For seven hours the Macedonian soldiers would not let the Albanian refugees cross the border. Then the Macedonian government allowed them in and they were relocated to stay in tents in a refugee camp. European government officials came and went. 'They put your name on a big board . . . If your name was there they would take your photo and check if you were healthy enough to travel on the plane. We put our name down to go to Australia.'

Then there was a smile at a memory of a moment in her story: 'We went down to look at the board, just me and my brothers, and then we saw our name . . . we were so excited!'

From Albania to Macedonia to Sydney to Adelaide and then to Melbourne. In Australia there was good food, bus trips and beaches. 'This was a happy time.' It was not difficult to make this a happy time. Albana came with her family. People were friendly. She was able to learn English and she was allowed to stay.

After staying in a camp in Melbourne for some time, Albana's family was told that they could live in Canberra. They got a house and she started school with her brothers. I know this well, because Albana's school is also my school. 'I was scared . . . It was my first school in Australia.' And then, with a laugh, 'Maybe the people were going to eat me!' I wrote this down. With both of us laughing, she said, 'No! Don't write that!' We laughed and smiled and decided to write it anyway.

Albana has made new friends, has got a part-time job and can now speak excellent English. She is in my art class at school and paints using beautiful colours. Together with our friends we paint so many pictures and maybe we use up more paint than everybody else in the school put together, but not to worry.

And what about the future? I asked.

'I want to be a doctor. But I'm not so sure. It's too soon to choose.'

So I guess we will have to wait and see. For now, we can laugh and smile and be happy. In smiling, however, there is a sadness for those who are unable to laugh as often as ourselves, and a tear might come to my eye when I think of those whose time in Australia is not as happy as Albana's was.

Albana has told me a little bit about herself, her family and her country. Sitting in the sun of our schoolyard I say thank you before the bell rings and we leave for class.

Taha's Story:
Adam's Version

by Adam Bennett, aged 12

Hi, my name is Taha and this is my story.

I was just a normal thirty-year-old woman. I lived in a country called Iraq. I had a job in a big office building, everything was great. But then there were the others. They came and took over the country. They put new laws down so that we couldn't talk our own language – it was terrible. My mum was an old lady so she did not worry about learning the new language. So she could only talk in secret.

One day I went to work early in the morning. I parked my car in its spot and took the lift to the top floor. Just as I reached my office, the phone rang. I ran in and just got it. It was mum. I had to talk to her in the forbidden language. She said she wanted me to buy her some bread and milk. My boss walked past. I slammed down the phone. He might have heard me but he was a good old man, so I thought he wouldn't turn me in to the secret police. I worked hard for the rest of the day on a new project. I decided it was time to go home. I went out to my car and hopped in. Two black cars came screeching up beside me. I was stuck, so I calmly walked up to ask them to move. When I reached their car two men jumped out and grabbed me. It was the secret police! I said to the men that I had done nothing wrong but they just hit me and kept on hitting me. They blacked out my eyes and put me in the car. They took me for a downhill drive. After ten minutes I blacked out and fell asleep.

When I woke up three days later I was in a dark damp room about two by two metres wide. It had a hole in the ground for a toilet and a tap above for a shower. The water in the tap was extremely cold. All the food and drink I got was a glass of cold water and a piece of stale bread. I would soak the bread in the water so that it became soft and easy to swallow. I had one blanket and a soft foam pillow for a bed. In the winter the temperature would drop to about two degrees but in the summer it got to around fifty degrees. In the summer I would sit under the cold dirty water of the shower.

Every day I would be woken very early, blindfolded and taken to a large room. In the room they would use a pulley to get me up to a large ceiling fan. My arms would be tied behind my back and hooked onto the fan. My body would overbalance and my head would face the ground. They would turn the fan on very fast for about two to three hours a day. When I got back to my room the glass of water and the piece of bread was ready.

Sometimes I would be interrogated and threatened. They would poke my eyes with needles and burn me with cigarette butts. Because of this I am now blind in one eye, have lower back problems and can't feel two fingers.

One night I was woken and taken from my room. They blindfolded me and pushed me into the car. We went for a very long downhill drive. It was very rocky and we took a lot of sharp turns. The car stopped. One of the men grabbed me and got out of the car. One of the others pulled off my blindfold. It was the first time I had seen light in six months! It was unbelievable.

There were thousands of little gaols. I was taken to one of them. They pushed me in and slammed the door. Two days later I was taken and given an electric shock. I became very sick and had to go to a special hospital for three weeks.

When I returned I was put in a different gaol. After two days in the gaol I realised that there was a small hole in the left hand side wall. I poured a cup of water down the hole. A young man yelled back. That young man became one of my best friends. We talked for hours at a time. He really helped me get through the devastation. The only problem was that I never got to see his face.

One day one of the guards heard us talking. He came and took that young man away. I battled on for another couple of days. Then after 200 days of hell, a soldier came and let me out. The sunlight hurt my eyes!

The war was on again. I ran into the hills. I found my way back to my family. I escaped to Jordan where I applied for a visa to Australia. It took two years to get on that plane.

I got a phone call after three months living in Australia. It was that young man. He had just got married to a beautiful lady in Japan. He gave me his email address. We mail each other every week and still to this day I have never seen that young man's face.

Taha's Story:
Chelsea's Version

by Chelsea June, aged 12

Hi, my name is Taha and I come from Iraq. I had a good life and a good family but then the war started between Iraq and Iran and things turned bad. So in the end when I was thirty I moved to Australia. Here's my story . . .

I was nine when we moved from North Iraq to Baghdad. My original language was Kurdish but the new laws were set and we were not allowed to talk Kurdish but had to talk Arabic. As my mother was an older woman she did not bother to learn Arabic. She only learnt words so that she could buy things.

Later on in my life I met my husband Saad and we had our first baby girl child named Larna.

One day, while my husband, Larna and myself were walking down the street, Larna told me to back up. She stopped at an apple stand and asked if she could have an apple. I could not say no to my child, so I asked if I could just have a single apple, but they didn't sell just single apples, they only sold kilos and half a kilo. So I asked for half a kilo which cost seventy-five cents and my husband's monthly pay was six dollars.

After a lot of trying, I finally got a job doing scientist work. One day while I was at work my mother rang to ask me if I could get milk and bread on the way home. My boss overheard me talking in a different language. I had to tell him what I was saying because he couldn't understand me. I could tell he didn't believe me.

At four o'clock I finished work and walked out to my car. I got in but found myself trapped. Two cars were blocking my car. I turned on the engine and waited for a while but they wouldn't move. So I got out of my car and tapped on their window and asked them to move. Next thing I know they were out of the car. They blindfolded me and then I was in the back of their car. I was so scared.

When they took the blindfold off me I was in a small room. It was so small that if I walked two steps I would hit the wall. There were no windows. The only thing in the room was a shower and a toilet which was ground level. I tried the shower and as I expected the water was as cold as cold, and dirty.

I fell asleep. I woke being shocked. The same men were back once again. They blindfolded me and when they took it off I was in a different room. Now I was really scared. They sat me in a chair and started asking me questions. If I didn't answer they would hit me. This happened every day for weeks and probably months. They started to do more things. Instead of using ashtrays they would put their cigarettes out on my hands. They also dipped needles in acid and put the needle in my eye. When this happened I was sent to a women's hospital for a couple of days. They also put clips on my tongue with electric shocks. Every couple of days they would hang me from the fan and I would most likely be up there for two hours. Every day I would just feel like dying in the gaol.

Then one day the men were back and blindfolded me as usual. When the blindfold came off, I was in an underground hole. I could tell it was up in the mountains by all the trees around the hole. There must have been at least 300 people. I thought that I was to stay here but all they were doing was picking up more people. When they left they blindfolded me again. When they took the blindfold off me, I was in the street. I could tell I was home!

I was so glad to see my husband and daughter. According to them I had been gone seven and a half months. I had had enough of this life and I made up my mind I was going to go to Australia. Two of my brothers lived in Newcastle working as dentists.

I then moved to Jordan. My brothers would send me $500 every month because I needed $5000 in my account. When I had all the money, I could then go to Australia.

When I got to Australia they took me on a tour of the city and asked questions about Australia. I had reading and writing tests and the points added up to 115, which got the visa to stay in Australia. When I got my visa I moved to Newcastle to live with my brothers for a while and then I moved to South Australia.

It has been sixteen years since I lived in Iraq. I sometimes get harassed in the street because people think I'm an Afghanistan spy after the September 11 bomb attack. They sometimes pull off my scarf and then start saying go back to where you came from and I just tell them that I am an ordinary person but I wear my scarf of religion.

I love Australia and I love living in South Australia and now I feel safe living here.

The Scar

by Alexandra Drakulic, aged 15

I could have written about absolutely anything since I was born in Bosnia and lived there during the war. I would have liked to tell you how my family escaped from Sarajevo and came to Australia, but since it is my best friend's birthday in seven days' time, I will tell you about her.

Well to start from the beginning, my best friend was Renata and I have known her ever since I could remember, or ever since I was able to know for myself. She lived just across from me, so we were always together. Renata was Muslim and I am Orthodox but this didn't matter. My sister used to tell us that we were joined at the hip. We went to pre-school together and we used to always pick fights with boys and then see which one had more bruises and scars. Well the reason that I am writing this is the scar on my leg reminds me of the war every time I look at it.

Renata and I started primary school and at that time the war had begun, but we were too young to understand what was going on and thought that this was only another day off school. In the beginning every one didn't actually believe that there was going to be a war, but in less than a week the city of Sarajevo was filled with army stations and barricades. At that time many people left but the majority stayed, thinking that this was only temporary. Within one month the power was cut and we had to walk about thirteen kilometres to get our water. Everyone had to help with this because the more people who went, the more water we could carry.

As the war was happening Renata and I used to play in my flat and her family would often stay at my house since we had a storeroom which was dug into the hill. At that time I realised that the war wasn't going to go away since there were more and more people coming into the city from surrounding villages. As kids we had our parents telling us all the things that we should do, but we always used to sneak out and go to our day-care centre or our school which had been turned into army centres. We had our little petty fights but we always managed to get over them.

But this was not to last.

As the peace treaty was signed with the UN and the Bosnian government, people were moving around more and we were allowed to play outside our flats during the day. While we were playing a game with all of the other kids who lived in sur-rounding buildings, one of the adults started yelling and all of a sudden the troops that were behind our flats started shooting. Every one jumped back and Renata and I hid under a car that was parked not far away from us. Then there was quiet and no one moved. It was as if time stopped for a split second. When I looked up I saw my cousin and Renata's mum yelling at us to get out from underneath the car. We climbed out quickly and started running towards the flats. To us this was funny and we were laughing.

When we reached my flats the booming started heavily and the shooting was so loud we had to cover our ears. As we were running in to the flats a grenade fell close to us. My cousin pulled me up off the ground, and as he was doing this I heard a loud scream which I was able to hear with my ears closed. As I turned around I felt a strong sharp pain in my leg and fell on the ground. Tarik, my cousin went to cover my eyes but I saw what I didn't want to believe. Renata was lying on the ground in a pool of blood, unconscious. Next to her were her mother and my parents. My cousin picked me up and then I realised that I had blood all over my leg and I couldn't feel it.

After that, it took me a while to realise what just happened, the fact that I had lost my best friend.

I was taken to the hospital because, on the impact of the explosion, a piece of metal got stuck in my leg and it needed to be taken out. When we reached the hospital I was in a lot of pain and I was feeling faint. But most of all I was scared of the hospital, because it is different when you hear about a war hospital and when you are actually in one. There was a lot of blood and injured people around, but what struck me was that there were dead people there that died before the doctors could get to them, and body parts everywhere.

At that time I passed out. When I woke up I was at home and the piece of metal was still there. One of my dad's friends was a vet before the war and he took it out with my sister's biology set.

The next day I saw Renata's mother and my mother talking and I came up to her and asked where was Renata. I was expecting her to tell me that she died but to my surprise she answered me with a smile on her face. Renata was still alive and in the hospital. That afternoon my mother took me to visit her and I was so happy to see her.

I spent the whole day talking to her about the things that we did before and what we were planning to do for my birthday, which was coming up.

The next day my mother came to by bedroom and sat on by bed. She told me that during the night Renata died from internal bleeding and that we were going to go to her funeral in a week. I was upset, but satisfied that I at least said goodbye in a kind of way to her. I didn't get to go to her funeral because the shooting was really bad.

When I was leaving Sarajevo, Renata's mother gave me her bracelet, one that Renata wore all the time.

Now all I have to remember one of my best friends is a bracelet and a scar on my leg.

The Blue Eyes that Grieve

by Zara Al-Hosany Al-Shara, aged 15

Zeinab is a sweet, slight and softly spoken girl. She seems just like any other twelve-year-old, with beautiful fair skin, a lovely smile, her head covered in the hijab. However there is something about Zeinab's big blue eyes that disturbs me. They look deep, tired . . . perhaps a little older than her twelve years. This is understandable when one realises the pain, suffering and loss that Zeinab has endured in the past year.

Zeinab is a refugee from Iraq. Like many, her father made the decision to flee his oppressive country in the search for peace, freedom and a better opportunity for his large family. However, this dream was to be the beginning of the end. A tragic end for Zeinab's family.

Australia was the destination, a long way to go, but this family of seven had suffered a great deal and lost everything. They had been a happy, wealthy family living in Najaf, a city in Iraq. The conflict between Saddam Hussein and the Iraqi people changed all that.

The Iraqi residents disliked Saddam as their president and wanted to change him. They held a strike that then started a war between Najaf and Karbala, another city. One of Zeinab's uncles got involved in the war as well. The family didn't take any action until seven years later, but the constant pressures and insecurity led to Zeinab's uncle deciding to leave Iraq and go to another country, where they could live in peace. Her father was always afraid of Saddam because his brother's family had left Iraq illegally and Saddam didn't know where they were. Zeinab's father was continually threatened in order to try to find out where his brother went. This placed them in even more danger.

Zeinab's family decided to leave Iraq and travel to Iran as refugees. Firstly they drove to Saudi Arabia and from there they caught an aeroplane to Iran. Moving to Iran wasn't a good idea because now they didn't have any money or a place to live and didn't even know Iranian. So they went to a place like the Salvation Army for help. The Salvos helped them a lot by providing them with food, clothing and shelter for six months. Finally her father found a job.

All of the family moved from Tehran to Quam because it was cheaper there. Her father's wage wasn't much, so they rented a cold and dark basement to live in. Zeinab and her sisters went to an Arabic school where there were mainly Arab refugees. The family were in such bad condition that sometimes they didn't even have enough money to buy food. They were so poor that they couldn't afford textbooks and usually slept without eating. They each owned only two sets of clothing, that's how bad their lifestyle was. Zeinab's father was saving up money to come to Australia. Her mother's brother lived in Australia and tried to sponsor them but it wasn't accepted. But her father so badly wanted to give his children a better future and he knew he could not do that living in Iran in such poor conditions, so the family would have to go to Australia illegally. Zeinab's father found a person who said that he could help them get to Australia. He said, 'If you want to go to Australia you have to take an aeroplane to Malaysia and there a man will come and put you on a boat that will take you to Indonesia. From there you have to take another boat to Australia.'

The problem was the cost. It would cost them US$1000 each person, not including the flight from Iran to Malaysia. They didn't have enough money so Zeinab's father borrowed US$8000 from his friends. He agreed to pay them back when he reached Australia.

Zeinab's father left Iran with his wife and five children. They were so happy that they were jumping for joy. Zeinab remembers how happy her parents were for the first time in a long time. The family was looking forward to a peaceful life in Australia with no tension or hardship.

Once they arrived in Malaysia it was all arranged. In Indonesia a man came up to them and took them to the boat that was meant to take them to Australia. Zeinab often has nightmares of the old battered boat and the look on her father's face when he saw it. 'It was very small and old. It seemed like it would sink at any moment,' she says. There were more than 400 people waiting to get on the boat when there was really meant to be half that. Zeinab remembers her father arguing with the man. He said, 'I am not going in this boat, it is a derelict boat.' The man replied, 'Go now or never! You are not getting your money back if you decide not to go. Besides, you'll be safe.' So Zeinab's father had no choice but to travel on that shabby boat. He was scared, Zeinab could tell, but they were happy at the same time.

In the middle of the long journey, while they were all sleeping, Zeinab's father woke up. He heard people screaming for their lives and he saw people jumping out of the boat, men, women, children and babies. It was chaos, confusion, hell. This part of Zeinab's story is quite horrifying and she cries softly when she relives the horror in her mind of that terrible night. Not many people in the boat knew how to swim so they either drowned or held onto pieces of the sunken boat. Zeinab, who was carrying her five-year-old brother, was holding onto a piece of wood. When her mother saw her she looked relieved but she was scared that Zeinab might drown. So she told Zeinab to hand her brother over. It was this decision Zeinab regrets dearly. Zeinab's mum drowned with her five-year-old son along with the seven-year-old boy she was already carrying. Zeinab remembers screaming and crying when she saw her mum drown with her younger brothers.

Later Zeinab saw her older sister drowning and calling for help. She tried to help but she couldn't. Just metres away she saw her father drowning with her nine-year-old sister. Within a few horrible minutes Zeinab's family members were swallowed up by the sea forever in front of her eyes. Darkness is all she remembers. When she awoke she saw none that she knew.

The next morning in a rescue boat there were twenty-five other desperate faces. She was alone . . . lost . . . orphaned. She remembers thinking that it wasn't a bad dream. The family . . . her beautiful mother . . . wonderful father and adorable brothers and sisters were gone. The boat took her back to Indonesia and they printed her photo in the newspapers. Zeinab's uncle saw her photo and requested the Australian government allow Zeinab to come and live in Australia. Fortunately they accepted her.

Today Zeinab lives with her uncle in NSW, a world away from misery. She doesn't have parents or sisters or brothers. She is completely lonely. Zeinab tries to see the positive things in life, but she says the memories and the loss will haunt her forever.

SPIRIT
REMAINED

'They did what they could to stay alive,
and then they played soccer.'

Kim's Story

by Helen Huynh, aged 15

'This isn't something you'd just forget,' he replied when I asked how vivid his recollections were. I remember how I leaned forward, pen in hand, not wanting to miss even a word. At that point I wasn't quite sure what to expect but I knew one thing. There was a history of struggle behind that boyish grin and that youthful temperament. I was attempting to conceive a reality so unlike my own that it seemed surreal.

On the night of 23rd April 1977, my uncle's journey began. He was standing on the dock, absorbing a scene of agitated people rushing back and forth around him. In his possession was a small bundle of his basic necessities, which he had strapped around his back. The only thing on him that was of any value was his mother's ring, which he wore cautiously on his finger. It was the only link he had to the family he left behind. My uncle was eighteen at the time.

On board the boat, about fifty other men and women sat wedged together, all sharing a look of quiet apprehension. They were aged from fifty to as young as fifteen, but each was there for different reasons. The atmosphere was dense with anxiety. It wasn't so much the fear of being caught, as their bribes had been wholeheartedly accepted, and the local government was turning a blind eye to their escape. Their fear was of the ocean; of dealing with the fact that something so alien had become their home.

But below the uneasiness was a lingering sense of relief. My uncle was conscripted to a war against the Chinese. Vietnam was now a Communist country. He was to fight for a cause which he had no loyalty to; and then he was to die a pointless, brutal death. But he was leaving it all behind. As the boat crawled deeper out to sea, my uncle made a vow to live. He knew that in order to survive mentally, he was going to have to block out all his excess emotions. He trained his mind into a state of detachment. From now on it was to only function systematically. But even in this, fate spared no mercy.

They were amateurs, prodding around in the dark with no plan, no expertise and no experience. On day one, the tired old engine stopped and they were stranded. Their compass busted, so they were lost as well. Then on further inspection, they found out that their Captain, a young man named Duc, was bogus. Duc had never driven a boat but was recklessly placed into that position. The bitter unfairness of this situation is laughable and my uncle recounts this incident with light humour.

Luckily though, they were able to work as a team. With bits of scrap they restored the engine to a semi-functioning standard. To keep track of direction, they followed the movement of the sun, and at night, the constellations of the stars. They knew that if they kept heading south, they'd eventually hit land. Unfortunately, this brief moment of bravado was short-lived. Any feelings of optimism were vanquished by day two, three, four, five, six, seven and eight.

Food rations hit a dangerously low level. The oldest were the most vulnerable. Their weakness made them sick, and after a few days they started dying. By this time though, death had become a tangible reality and the survivors accepted it quietly. There was never an uncontrolled despair, despite knowing that they could be dead the next day. The irony was that exhaustion was what kept my uncle's mind together.

On the eighth day, those who were still alive saw land. Some cheered, some cried. The important thing was, everybody saw hope again. And then the boat broke in two. They were a hundred metres from shore and not everybody could swim. Sharp corals framed the island bed, savaging the skin of those who dared to cross it. My uncle and a few others had to lap over them several times to rescue as many people as they could.

Finally, gasping for breath, dizzy and choking with salt water, my uncle dragged the last person to safety. He clambered further onto shore and collapsed. His body was stained with blood. The survivors lay there for some time, not daring to open their eyes, hardly believing that they were actually alive.

As my uncle lay there on the sand, he dreamt. It was a dream that was to recur again many times over the course of his life. In his dream he was trapped back at home. He was holding a gun, preparing for battle. But something was wrong. With mounting frustration he realised that he didn't want to kill people, nor did he want to die so worthlessly. There was a great life waiting for him to live, big things he yearned to achieve. Desperation engulfed him, suffocating him.

'To think you're doomed,' my uncle said, 'and then waking up to see the sun, sand and trees, the feeling is unspeakable. You appreciate your freedom so much more and with that mentality you can take on the world.'

When they woke up the next day, a new chapter started. They were in Indonesia on one of the tropical islands. The sun was a healthy and steady twenty-eight degrees, and the jungle was thick and waiting to be explored. Immediately they filed into groups of roughly six to eight people but everyone made an effort to pitch in, eager to do something useful for the group.

The coconut trees towered up ten to fifteen metres high and my uncle, who was exceptionally fit, used to climb and pick them to share around with the others. But they needed nutrients, so out came the fishing hooks, rods, nets, and scuba masks. They also needed shelter, so a hut was built out of logs and leaves. At this point in time it sounds a bit like a camping trip or the reality show 'Survivor'. But it wasn't like that at all. You didn't play the game for money or for your joy. You played the game for your life.

On that island, if you didn't cut it, if you were weak, you'd die. If you sat on a sand mound there would probably be a body underneath. Anything you ate or touched was completely at your own risk but you took the risks anyway because there was no other choice.

Hunger was a driving force; it made you do things you wouldn't normally dare to do. When your body cries out for food you'd do anything to satiate the need. You would follow a turtle into the depths of the night to locate its eggs. You would eat oysters, realise they're poisonous, and keep eating them in the hope that you might become immune.

One night, my uncle was awoken by a series of screams. He and two friends got up and went to see what the commotion was about. What they saw was a three and a half metre snake. My uncle backed away cautiously but he heard a whisper from one of his friends, 'Kill! Kill it!'

And that was the way life had become. If anything moved, you ate it. Life was tough and yet somehow they didn't become brutal, heartless and greedy beings. The Vietnamese are a playful people. They did all they could to stay alive and then they played soccer. The bond and sense of companionship between them was impenetrable. Even though they were extremely poor they always looked out for each other, sharing whatever food they could collect, often giving them out to the elders.

As for the lovely hut they built; it was effectively useless. When it rained, water seeped through the many gaps and gushed down upon them. The weather got remarkably cold after dark and it was impossible to sleep on most nights. Strangers would huddle together, sharing warmth. They would stand there, shivering and rubbing their arms, waiting for day to dawn.

Amidst all these hardships, a great sense of spirit remained. Resources were limited but they made the best out of the little that they had. Nobody ever complained because even on the worst days they were able to console themselves in the knowledge that at least they were living, free men.

Eventually, the Indonesian Government acknowledged them and sent aid in the form of food, blankets and plastic (for shelter). They were relocated to a better island. As a result of this, fewer people died, but overall they weren't much better off. Starvation was still a problem, as was boredom.

The second problem was tackled deftly on this new island. There was an assortment of skills between them and so classes were started up. The types of classes ranged from English to sports to chess. My uncle, who was training to become a PE teacher when he was conscripted, ran a vigorous, daily exercise routine.

To tackle the first problem, hunger, my uncle made a huge decision. He spent days thinking about it and on the fifth day he traded in his mother's ring for cash. With hindsight he concludes: 'No matter how hard things get, there's always a business to run – even if you only make peanuts.'

He wanted a long-term solution so he made one. There were people with money who wanted shelter but had no accessible manpower. He collated a crew of twenty young men and added himself into the equation. Before long he was supporting a booming shelter-building business. The Indonesian shops in the local area were delighted about this explosion of customers and my uncle developed quite a reputation. Through the risk that he took, he stopped being perpetually hungry. He wasn't immune to disease, however, as life was still tough. He caught malaria.

One and a half years later, when he was nineteen, the long-awaited miracle happened. The Australian officials paid a visit, offering places in their country. At this time my uncle had recovered from malaria. He applied and went through a series of interviews. Two weeks later he became an Official Australian Citizen. All his hardship had paid off; he was going to the West.

To understand what went through his mind you have to know his character. As a youngster he was mischievous and disobedient, constantly in trouble for fighting with the local boys, gambling (and cheating) with the old lady next door or skipping school to go fishing. But the hardships that he faced over this short amount of time ensured that he was to change; he had now grown into a mature and responsible young man.

Through this though, hidden aspects of his personality emerged, like his instinctive need to be challenged, his ambition, and his will to succeed. He was extremely grateful to get the opportunity of becoming a part of Australia. He wanted to contribute to the country that had adopted him. My uncle made a new vow; he was to be an asset to it and make a real difference.

Before my uncle boarded the plane, he took off all his outer garments and even his shoes. He left them behind for his best friend, who needed them more than he did. He gave his friend a final hug, punched him playfully on the shoulder before ascending the stairs.

Wearing only a dirty, frayed singlet and limp shorts, owning nothing of value, ('Why should I bring peanuts to Australia?') he made a strict contrast to the passengers on board. He looked at his ticket and made way to his given seat, aware of being watched. It just so happened that it was beside a neat and conservative looking old man. Fortunately, my uncle had attended a few of the English classes back on the island.

He asked, 'Sir, what do you have for lunch in Australia?' Aside from wanting to make conversation, my uncle was also curious to know what Westerners ate, because apparently they didn't eat rice or noodles. To this day, my uncle is able to recollect the feeling of heated embarrassment. The man turned around impatiently and said, 'Hamburgers,' My uncle, having no idea what that was, laughed and nodded, feeling extremely stupid. He sat quietly for the rest of the ride, but his mind was buzzing with realisation.

His journey was far from over. The loneliness hit him and he realised how isolated he was and how different the struggle ahead was going to be. He had no money, no education, no connections and, in light of his recent discovery, no English either. All he had was himself but he was determined to make something out of that. Immersed in his own thoughts he let the plane sail peacefully towards his new home: Australia.

Today my uncle owns a chain of successful framing outlets. Although he works extremely hard, he has kept his sense of adventure and love of sport. He has three sons who carry his boisterousness, and lives with his wife in Melbourne. He still likes fishing and has bought a holiday house for this reason – he has stopped climbing coconut trees, however.

Since coming to Australia, he has won several tennis and iron man competitions and also participated in various outdoor activities, like parachuting, hang-gliding, scuba diving and archery. 'To see what life has to offer,' he said.

Although content now, he recounts his tough road to the top, where at one point he balanced three jobs at the one time, having only a few hours sleep in between. He recalls the annoyance of not being able to speak English and owning nothing, but at the end of the day, is wholesomely glad that he took the road that he did.

Life. You Never Know What's Ahead of You. Never

by Mina Hami, aged 16

My name is Mina and I've been living in Australia for about five years. I was born on 5th April 1986 in northern part of Iraq. Life in my homeland was very hard, in order to survive you actually had to finish school with a very high HSC mark to get a professional job that makes enough money for living.

I come from a very educated family. My dad and mum are teachers of biology and chemistry. That's why for me it's hard to leave school and choose what I want to do other than be a doctor, engineer or teacher. So I have to finish school with a high HSC mark.

But it was in April 1992 when my dream of becoming a doctor was ruined and taken away. It was War again. The government of Iraq was persecuting the Kurdish people in northern Iraq where I lived. I waited anxiously with my family in our home as helicopters flew across the house bombing the places next to our suburb, a tragedy which made the whole town escape to the mountains of Turkey.

I was six years old then, when one morning, I got up and heard noises coming from my house. I rushed up to my mum and asked 'What's going on Mum? What's happening?' Mum said 'Come on, honey, get in the car, I'll explain later.' So I ran and got in the car. Mum said 'We're going to the mountains of Turkey.' 'Why?' I asked. She replied with a sad, soft, smooth voice and a very worried look, 'Because, do you see all the bombing that's been happening here, we're running away from it to keep you and your sister safe and in peace with no danger, so we're going to the mountains of Turkey.' When she said those words I looked in her eyes, and I could feel and sense the terror and fear in her. It was like she wasn't sure of what she was doing or saying.

By the time we reached the mountains I watched hundreds of people running away with their kids and family. It was a disaster coming true. I mean, I've seen a disaster and danger happening on television but this one was a real live situation happening right in front of my eyes. I could see it, feel it and touch it, just like a witness in a crime scene. It was freezing and it was pouring rain and the ground had turned to mud and snow. Sometimes my parents would carry my sister for half an hour and swap and carry me for the other half an hour. It was a desperate time. It was so hard. We were suffering from cold and shortage of food and drink. Something we never ever imagined would occur had happened in our lovely town, by our own government.

In the mountains we would all try to be close to each other, so we wouldn't lose one another and try to hope and wish for a miracle to happen. That we would get to Turkey and be rescued as soon as possible. I remember my dad asking people how much further to get to Turkey and some people would say half an hour, the others would say one or two days. The truth, no one, really no one, knew how long or how much further to get to Turkey. But it was amazing how everybody tried not to give up and kept on moving. To me it felt like I was playing a guessing game, guessing will I survive and get there safe and sound or will I just die here and become this left fossil to never be discovered ever again?

The only thing I enjoyed out of it was that I got to sit on a horse. I remember my uncle said to me, 'Are you tired of walking?' I replied 'Yeah. I am very tired and I don't think I can walk anymore.' He said 'Well. Get yourself ready because you're about to get a ride!' When I heard these words I jumped up and down saying, 'Are you serious uncle?' He replied, 'Oh yeah! Because you are going to get a ride on a horse!' and I screamed as loud as I could, 'Woohoo! I'm going to ride a horse. Woohoo!' So I got to sit on a horse for a little while with my uncle at the front and my sister at the back. That moment felt like I was this princess who got rescued by prince charming.

However the sad thing was that I saw people getting sick and dying and all I could do was just stand, watch, cry and start walking again. There was nothing, nothing anyone could do to help except to give sympathy. Throughout this unforgettable, torturing and miserable journey my family and I walked and slept for seventy-two memorable, harsh and emotional days. We finally reached Turkey, were rescued and were sent back to our little town called Dohuk.

In 1996 my family decided it was time to leave the country for a new and better life for me and my sister. A life that could build a career for us with peace and freedom. A country that is able to recognise the rights of a human being and is able to count the votes for legal and political rights. So we left our homeland and headed to that disastrous place Turkey again. We stayed in Turkey for about three years waiting for an exemption from the Australian embassy and thanks to heavenly God and Australia we did get a straight 'YES'.

In 1998 in October we reached Australia. At that time I felt I was in this whole new world. A world full of happiness and excitement. It was like the beginning of a new life. Like the opening of a new chapter in a book. A life that can build my future with peace and not war.

The airport at Sydney is not really a pretty place. It's very busy and surrounded by factories and warehouses, but to me it's the most beautiful and wonderful place in the entire world because of what it represents – my freedom.

Somehow we managed to settle in, but trust me it wasn't easy. Looking for a place with the difficulty of not knowing much English is the hardest thing to do. It was like running around in circles.

The worst thing I faced was that first day of school. The scariest day in my entire life. The thing that made me get scared was not knowing how to speak English. The fear of going to class was so strong that my ears and cheeks went red just like a tomato. But fact is, after learning how to speak English, I feel like a native Australian. I just love it!

Another difficulty I faced was finding friends and getting to know them. People in Australia are friendly but are very different to where I came from. It was very hard for me to try and open up to friends and get to know them. I felt this way because I was scared of what they might think of me. A freak! Just because I think different to what they think. My sister and I used to hang around together. I remember that one day we were sitting by ourselves eating lunch, and suddenly we saw this girl coming towards us who said, 'Hey girls, would you like to hang around with me and my friends?' I replied with a big smile on my face, 'Yes, thank you. That's very nice of you.' Since then, even though I changed schools I am still friends with that girl and she is my best friend.

Reality in Australia, the attitude, the way of living and honesty is so different from where I came from. As they always say, Australia has freedom and that's what makes Australia a whole lot different from Iraq. The word 'Freedom' does not exist there. I managed to fit in with friends and the lifestyle and I am continuing to manage my future, hopefully with a successful education so I would live the life that my parents brought me here to have. From the day I was born until the day I die.

Today my family and I are citizens; we are Australians. We go to school, my family pays tax, we are loyal to the country that gave us liberty and hope. I am very thankful for everything this country has done for me and my family. Coming to Australia is the best thing that ever happened to me in my entire life. Knowing this is the destiny and opportunity to fulfil my dreams, every day I wake up and look at beautiful sunshine. I think and wonder what is still ahead of me. I guess this is life, you never know what is ahead of you. Never.

Out of Italy

by Rosie Clare Giudici, aged 12

'Excuse me,' asked a man with a troubled frown, 'do you know a boy here called Sergio?' The young boy looked up into the man's eyes and replied, 'Yes, that's me.' For the first time in nine years Sergio looked into the eyes of his father.

In 1948 Sergio, who was ten years old, arrived in Melbourne with his mother. He had travelled for twenty-eight days on an Egyptian boat called the Al Sudan from Marseilles in France. They had fled Italy to be reunited with Sergio's father, Bruno, who had fled the fascist regime nine years earlier.

Life in Italy during the early 1940s had been difficult. Italy's leader, Mussolini, was forcing Italians to join up and fight with Hitler's army. Bruno opposed this and feared being persecuted by Mussolini for not joining the army. As a result Bruno and his brother, Ugo, along with many other men from the surrounding villages fled Italy and travelled to countries such as France, America and Australia to seek refuge. On arriving in Australia Bruno was interned along with other people of Italian and German descent and worked for nine years on construction projects around Australia. After the war he found work in Tasmania on the hydro-electric projects.

Sergio grew up in a village called Sernio in the Northern Italian Alps, in the region of Valtellina. Here he herded the cows up into the Alps every summer to fatten them on the luscious grass. He helped milk them and make cheese. He learnt how to butcher meat and make sausages and how to grow grapes. He attended elementary school and skied to school in winter with his friends.

Sergio witnessed the outstanding courage of his mother, who after the war had tried on several occasions to get on a boat that would take them to Australia. They had to travel down through the mountains and all the way to Marseilles, the port in France. Every time they arrived, they were not allowed on. Then one day, whilst waiting in Marseilles, his mother heard on the radio that a ship was coming into berth. She raced off to the ticket office and bought two tickets before anyone else and this time she knew she had made it.

After arriving in Port Melbourne and being reunited with each other again, Bruno, Elsa and Sergio hopped on another boat and sailed off to Tasmania. Once there they were then transferred to a remote destination in the Central Highlands of Tasmania called Butler's Gorge. They had a small house in the village and everyone was exceptionally friendly. There was not a very large variety of food but before long the immigrants began to arrange for the varieties that Italians know and love to be imported. The family was so happy to be reunited again. They lived in hope and faith in God.

Gradually the number of Italian and other European families increased in Butler's Gorge. Sergio attended primary school there for two years. After only one year at primary school, Sergio won the school prize for English! When he reached high school he boarded at New Town High School and later became house master.

After graduating from high school Sergio enrolled at the University of Tasmania where he became one of the founding students of St John Fisher College, a catholic residential college.

While at a youth function at the Springs Hotel on Mt Wellington, Sergio met a woman called Rossalyn Hundt. Rossalyn had come down from Queensland on a working holiday. These two romantic people fell in love and decided to get married. That same year Sergio won the Rhodes scholarship, the first migrant person in Tasmania to do so. He studied a PhD in Engineering at Oxford University in England for three years, and for three years Rossalyn waited patiently for him to return. On 18th January 1964 they were married.

After returning from Oxford he was employed by the Hydro-Electric Commission, based in Hobart. One of his major achievements and first big projects was the design of the Gordon Dam, a concrete arch dam.

While working for the Hydro, he pioneered the design of concrete faced rock filled dams and his expertise in that area was in demand all over the world. Later in his career he became the founding manager of the consulting arm of the Hydro and in this role he travelled extensively on the business of major engineering projects, in countries such as China, Laos, Indonesia and the Philippines. Sergio was also involved in the Italian community, helping these people with immigration issues and local concerns.

He was a great friend of Archbishop Guilford Young and James McCauley, the famous Tasmanian poet and English professor with whom he organised many seminars and conferences. Sergio attended mass at St Mary's Cathedral and was very involved in the parish. He was very devoted to his faith and the Church.

But to concentrate only on his professional career would be to only reveal half the man. Sergio loved hosting celebrations with family and friends and was never happier than when opening a bottle of wine to share with his four sons and three daughters.

In early 2000 he retired from the Hydro after thirty-seven years' service but still maintained an active role in the engineering community. On 27th April 2002, whilst consulting in New Zealand he became suddenly ill and died. He was sixty-four years old.

This beautiful man was my grandad and I'll always hold the fondest memories in my heart. The way he used to nibble his grandchildren's ears; wrestle with the toddlers on the floor; blow raspberries in our ears; slump asleep in his armchair after Christmas feasts. I will especially remember wonderful food and the bottles of wine he would open, the way he used to sing louder than the opera on the record, and the way he just loved every minute he spent with his family.

He is sadly missed by his wife, mother, sister, seven children and their husbands and wives, and by his thirteen grandchildren.

Uhuru

by Simon Pitt, aged 16

As the battle started, mortars, grenades and machine-gun bullets tore into a line of 1200 government troops. Clouds of smoke and panicked birds billowed from the ground below. Standing under an African thorn tree, the rebel commander looked on, as the carnage unfolded on the Sudanese savannah. It is 1983, and the first day of death had begun, ending a nine-year ceasefire in Africa's largest country, and longest war.

Meanwhile, in the remote town of Bor, buried deep in southern Sudan, Chol traced circles in the sand which dominates the landscape. A young man wielding a sub-machine gun walked past Chol's hiding spot, beads of sweat glistening on his forehead under the legendary Saharan sun. Chol was well used to the formidable presence of militiamen around his hometown, but nonetheless, he felt a chill run down his spine as this enormous specimen of a man marched by. This man was not like the others, but a black militiaman in the pay of Sudan's Arab regime, further symptomatic of the latest outbreak of hostilities between the Islamic north and Christian south.

Walking through the park, his brothers' light-hearted chatter reverberated down the street. It was then that Chol heard the distant throbbing of aeroplane propellers. Only nine years old, Chol had not witnessed the turbulent end of Britain's influence in his country, nor the harrowing beginnings of Sudan's civil war, but even so, Chol knew that the ominous whirring he heard approaching meant no good.

It was on that day that the bombing began. Soviet-owned planes swept across the small city, leaving in their wake a path of devastation. Pilots would sweep so low that their unfaltering faces, hardened by government propaganda, were visible in the cockpit. Chol hurried home from the park, petrified by the images that now filled his head. All too aware of the dangers of staying, Chol's father immediately instructed him and his three younger brothers, to run.

Chol fled on foot, and amidst the confusion, he was separated from his brothers, whom he would not see for many years to come. It soon became clear that escaping would be hard and although Chol began his flight from persecution with hundreds of others, he had to go on as if he were alone. Of those he began with, many did not make it. Realising they could expect no sympathy, they wearily pulled themselves from the track to die.

They did not travel on the road, because of the constant threat posed by the presence of militiamen, both those of the government and the many local warlords, and so instead they traced a treacherous path through the savannah. Food and water were short, and the fugitives strictly rationed what they could carry in makeshift containers on their heads. Chol had no shelter, no money, no clothes other than what he had on, and had to forage for the little food and water he got. The hundreds Chol went with did not offer him any help – each person struggled making their own way – but they did offer him someone to follow, and this gave him hope.

It took three long months to reach the Ethiopian border. Hostile mercenaries were rampant. They would take whole crowds trying to cross the border and order them to hand over money and valuables of any kind or be killed.

In spite of the odds, young Chol finally arrived at Dimma one day late in 1983. Hemmed in by seemingly boundless expanses of desert on all sides, this was the day that Chol entered a refugee camp and became a refugee. Chol came to the camp alone, and at just nine years of age self-sufficiency was a characteristic deeply imbued in his character. He was briefly screened, before being pushed out into the unwelcoming world that was the Dimma refugee camp.

The conditions in the camp were nothing short of horrific. To begin with, the time Chol spent there, he spent alone. For the first few nights, he slept on a cramped and hardened piece of earth beneath the starry expanse of African sky which spread out above him. Chol soon set about constructing himself a small mud hut. It was hard work and he laboured alone for days under a violent sun to complete the hut that for the next ten years, he would make his home.

And for ten years, the yellow dunes would reign supreme, determined to fetter his attempts at moving forward. The yellow sand permeated everything, working its way through gaps in the walls and roof, each morning leaving a thin film of fine yellow grains around the place where his head had been. He would feel it against his face and in his hair and in the inside of his mouth too. The nights were cold.

There was no sense in talking to anyone about things. Everyone was in the same position. They all just wandered about like ghosts, the desert looming either side of them. There were crowds everywhere, but everyone was alone.

One day Chol discerned that everything was gradually changing for the better. This was the day it was announced that rudimentary schooling was to commence for the children in the camp. Long deprived of the simple joys of childhood, it was the first excitement Chol had felt in many months.

To begin with, they were divided into classes of fifty, took their lessons under what little shelter the thorn trees around the camp could offer and wrote with charcoal on cardboard packaging. Soon Chol was fortunate enough to be allocated a sponsor, and was then allowed to go to a school in town. Here he completed his education whilst living in the refugee camp. Chol wanted to pursue medicine, but could not afford the prohibitive costs of study, and so he went on to do a teaching diploma. It was at that time, in the horrendous conditions of Dimma refugee camp that Chol met Ariet.

Ariet's first husband had been killed some years earlier, and she was living as a widow when she first arrived at the camp. Their courtship was brief: an Ethiopian refugee camp was no place for romance.

The camp's conditions were still unimaginably horrific, but Chol had finally found strength through the happiness his wife's companionship gave him. Chol's newly-wed bride soon announced that she was expecting their first child, and several months after that, they brought a beautiful young girl, Hasana, into the world.

Chol's lowly mud hut in Dimma refugee camp was hardly a proper place to bring up a child, and come 1994, war had broken out anew in Ethiopia in the wake of Eritrea's recent secession. Security at Dimma crumbled in the following weeks, and Chol, along with Ariet, Hasana, and fifteen other friends from the camp decided to move on.

Thus began the soul-destroying journey which lay ahead of him. As with his escape from Sudan over ten years earlier, Chol, his wife and friends fled on foot. Again, they could not follow the roads for danger of persecution, and again they had no money, water or food. This time, however, Chol was charged with the added responsibility of protecting his wife and six-month-old daughter, and they were ill-prepared for the conditions ahead.

The water was bad; any that was found had to be drunk and that which was left over, they had to carry on their heads in whatever container they could fashion at the time. En route, many were plunged into a ruthless cycle of poor health and those who were relatively well had to care for those who were not. Many amongst the group had badly blistered feet and everyone removed their clothing to use as bandages. In the cold and hungry nights, and the hot and hungry days, Hasana cried hopelessly for food as Chol carried her in a makeshift sling on his back. This continued for three and a half months as the small group walked towards their final destination, the Kenyan border.

When they finally reached the border, the Kakuma refugee camp, they were not alone. Indeed, there were 96,000 other refugees from the neighbouring countries of Ethiopia, Somalia and Sudan – all thrust into turmoil by the political climate that pervades much of Africa to this day. Here, Chol was tearfully reunited with three of his brothers, Artem, Kabira and Abraham, whom he had neither seen nor been able to communicate with for many years. Moreover, it was the first time that Chol had ever met his thirteen year-old brother, Abraham. This was a moment of great joy and pride for Chol. All the same, not all was well at Kakuma.

Without sufficient food, water or shelter, tensions between the hundreds of ethnic groups ran high, and affrays were a regular occurrence in the camp. Likewise, situated close to the Kenyan border, the number of militiamen from neighbouring countries was of epidemic proportions. Hundreds of innocent refugees were killed – for their gold teeth, their Christianity, or for no reason at all.

At the camp, Chol and Ariet were processed by the UNHCR and so began their uphill battle to be accepted in a Western country as refugees seeking political and religious asylum. While it would seem that for many others of the 96,000 in his company, providence was not on their side, Chol was fortunate enough to be processed relatively quickly, waiting only three years for Australia's eventual notification of acceptance. Within a few short weeks, the Australian government had arranged the necessary flights and Chol was embarking on the most important journey of his life.

On his arrival in Australia in 1998, Chol was sent to Hobart, Tasmania, with his wife and child. Soon afterwards, he moved to

Launceston, where he could pursue a nursing degree at the University of Tasmania, fulfilling his lifelong dream to work in medicine. Two years on, with the help of a Launceston church, Chol was again reunited with three of his brothers, after successfully petitioning for their processing on compelling compassionate grounds.

With the support of his church and friends, Chol, a self-motivated student, quickly picked up English, his fourth language, and will soon finish his nursing degree. He hopes to remain in Launceston, his home, where Chol and Ariet have had three more delightful children – all of whom are proud to call Australia home.

Even now, Chol's life is clouded by uncertainty. Recently, he learnt of a devastating militia attack at Kakuma refugee camp. After several painful weeks of not knowing, and desperately trying to contact foreign embassies and family, it was confirmed that Ariet's sister was killed in the senseless massacre.

Chol's next challenge is to achieve reunion with Ariet's children from her first marriage, who are still in Africa. They have not yet been processed by the UNHCR for consideration for refugee status in Australia since they are not living in a refugee camp. The problem is complicated by Ariet's father's determination to prevent them from entering a refugee camp, since the inherent danger is just too great.

In spite of all he has experienced, Chol is remarkably optimistic in his approach to life, and his commitment to asylum seekers and wider community is a testament to his burning desire to live, and make a difference in the world. Chol's story is one of survival over immense circumstantial forces against it, and today, Chol feels immeasurably grateful to the Australian government for the opportunities they have afforded him and his family. His only wish is that the privilege of sharing in his new country – our country – could be extended to more people, who like him, have suffered beyond most people's comprehension.

Life

by Ghulam-e-Ali, aged 19

Life is defined as 'the period when a person is born, till his/her death.' It means the time starts when a person is born and the time stops or finishes on death. In this period many difficulties, problems, and hard times come like the waves. To pass or to face all of these problems, difficulties, and hard times successfully is called life.

Life is not to turn off your head from all of these problems, difficulties and hard times. We are in a cycle of time. Those are not run with the time, time crossed them it never stops. In addition time passes 'Good' or 'Bad.' It is unstoppable. So it's better to pass the time well and poorly than bad. To stand bravely with courage and face the challenge is life.

I am an Afghan refugee. I am the eldest of five children. I was born on 1st January 1983 in a village of Ghazni. I came to Australia on 7th March 2001. I was in Curtin Detention Centre for approximately thirteen months and then came to Brisbane. I am very keen to study so I gained admission to high school. From there I finished my English, Maths and Science with high achievements, on 27th March 2002. I would like to be a software engineer.

I can speak seven languages, which are Hazargi, Dari, Farsi, Pashtoo, Urdu, Hindi and English. I was the best athlete of my district. I like Kung fu and boxing.

The story which I wrote is about my own life.

Today is the 105th golden day of my life that I have enjoyed free, physical and mental freedom. I came to Brisbane from Curtin Detention Centre, WA, on 20th March 2002. I have two brothers and two sisters. My father, Mohammad Hussain, was the professor of English literature in Kabul University, and my mother, Zahra, was a busy housewife. I came to Australia in 2001, although my journey of struggling started when I was only three years old.

In the beginning of 1979, the Soviet Union came to Afghanistan. While passing through Ghazni, they tried to conquer Jaghori (one of the literate, populated and advanced areas of Hazara-jat, the area occupied by Hazara people) but they failed. The Soviet army diverted their way at that time but they came again and attacked Jaghori in 1986 (according to the Afghan calendar, by the end of 1364).

The Soviet army had advanced artillery, while against them, the locals of the district had nothing. The entire district had nothing. So before taking any further action, the elders of the township decided to surrender, because all they had to fight with were wooden bars and some rusted rifles from the World War II era. So to save the maximum damage the group of elders held a table talk with the Russian military leaders. From that day till now no one knew where they went. Villagers think that the Russian military killed them.

A few days after that tragedy, the Soviet army started the fearful fighting. They killed hundreds of innocent people. They spread thousands of mines around the town. Till now on the Loman Mountains (a series of high mountains in central Jaghori district) no one likes to go there, even for their lost animals, because of mines. Unwillingly, the local people, for their defence, came out and made a 'Hezb' (group or party) by the name of Hezb-e-Sholly. Hundreds of locals were killed. From my village, Baba, west of Sang-e-Masha (major town of Jaghori and magistrate office area) tens of people were killed. Among them the first *shaheed* (killed) was my paternal uncle Mohammad Ali, who was buried near the main mosque of Baba village.

Hundreds of families escaped from town to other countries to protect their lives. The tanks even came to my sub village. They destroyed many houses and a part of our house was also destroyed. At that I was time only three years old with my brother Abbas, approximately one year old, and my little sister Mariyam, only two months. My father decided because of these circumstances to leave the country. So my family moved to Pakistan.

It was the winter of 1986, when we came to Quetta city, which is near to the border of our country. Thousands of Afghan refugees were already there. My father first went to one of the refugee camps, but instead of helping, the workers totally ignored us. They mistreated my father, and did not give us any kind of shelter or food. Why? Because, overwhelmingly important in their mind, we were Hazara and Shia Muslim and they were Pashtun and Sunni. So unwillingly, like others, we went to Barori (ten kilometres west of the city and one of the muddy and backward areas with a majority of refugees). We rented a room and small shop with the money that my father had taken in a hurry from Afghanistan. My father bought some foodstuffs and started a grocery shop.

For the moment we thought that we had saved our lives and we could spend some relaxing time with sleepy nights. But after a few days many problems hit us. On one side were the owner of the house and neighbours, and on the other side were the policemen. The locals thought that due to the Afghan people their country was going backward, that drugs were being spread in their country due to Afghans, and God knows, many things more. They looked at us like *shouther* (the Untouchables of the Hindu religion), worked us like animals and even their children were not allowed to play with us. The police also harassed us. We had no choice except to survive.

Time passed and we spent many years there. I helped my father in the shop and my father taught me our religion as well as some English and Maths. We hardly survived on the income of the shop and suffered from every day tensions. Many times when anyone abused my mother or father, I started fighting with them. A question came to my mind every time about why these things were happening. We were also human and of equal value like others.

In 1991 the Pashtuns attacked our village and killed more then two hundred villagers. They destroyed almost half of our village and farms. In this brutal war it was clear that Pashtuns would never be friendly throughout their lives.

We had left in our village our maternal uncle to look after our lands and home. He was a member of Hezb-e-Wahdad party (the biggest Hazara party). So when the Taliban came and attacked Bamiyan (a province in Afghanistan and the major area of Hazara-jat), he was *shaheed* (killed) by the Taliban while defending the Bamiyan province. He was the only man left in Afghanistan from our family and after he was killed, his family was alone there. So for that family, our lands, and our situation in Pakistan, my father decided to go back. That was a very difficult decision, but I think my father had no choice again and we went back.

I was back with my family in my village after eight years. I was very happy because for the first time in my life I saw respect, sincerity and prosperity. I was going to the Shohada School. I saw pure hearts full of sincere feelings. But that would not last forever. This time the Taliban regime came to our district in early 1996. Once again the elders decided to surrender and not to fight with them. It was the only district of Hazara-jat that surrendered to the Taliban. After the surrender and control of the district the Taliban collected the weapons from villagers. They promised not to interfere with religious and personal affairs. But after eight months the Taliban extremists started their rule. They even killed those people who did not obey them in different ways like tying them to rockets and firing them, and hammering large metals spikes in their heads.

Their respect for women was zero. The Taliban perfected subjugation. In his day, the Prophet Mohammad (peace be upon him) was a support for women's rights. The doctrine he laid out as the revealed word of God considerably improved the status of women in 7th century Arabia. Islamic law made the education of girls a sacred duty and gave women the right to own and inherit property. Mohammad (peace be upon him) even decreed that sexual satisfaction was a woman's entitlement.

Of course, ancient advances do not mean that much to women fourteen centuries later if reform is, rather than a process, a historical blip subject to reversal. While it is impossible, given their diversity, to paint one picture of women living under Islam today, it is clear that the religion has been used in most Muslim countries not to liberate but entrench inequality. The Taliban represents an extreme.

They insisted that we do everything according to their will and wishes. They monitored key persons like doctors, engineers, and scholars, and accused them in different ways, believing the basic danger was due to these people. Then they requested a donation of young people from every sub-village. No one liked to go and fight against their own Hazara, and kill them or be killed by them and by the Taliban. If some fortunately survived, the Taliban would kill them straight away just so that news of their deaths came to the area. In addition, the Taliban stopped people getting an education for their younger generation and did not allow the Hazara people to follow and practice their religion.

When the Taliban came to my house, they accused my father of being involved with and supporting Hezb-e-Wahdad, because they knew that my maternal uncle was the key member. Hezb-e-Wahdad was supported financially by my family and the Taliban were compelling us to pay them a large amount of money, otherwise they would take me away and send me to the frontline to fight. My father paid them several times, but a few months later they started to harm and mistreat my father too. It was inconvenient to pay them every few weeks to save my life and my father managed with difficulty to keep me. So he decided to send me out to a safe country.

My father managed to find a smuggler and I was told to go to Australia, I came to Pakistan by car, and from Pakistan to Singapore and Indonesia by aeroplane. I faced many problems and difficulties during this long journey but all of them are nothing compared to the sixteen days at sea.

On 28th February 2001 I started my risky journey by boat to Australia. That night the thunder roared, the rain started and the waves smashed the boat. Due to darkness on the boat I did not understand the situation fully and sat in one of the corners. I didn't sleep the whole night due to engine pollution too. I vomited many times.

Next day when the sky cleared up, the sun shone again. I was shocked to see the condition and size of the boat and the number of people on it. There were probably 190 people in that boat and the length of the boat was not more than thirteen metres. That boat was eighty years old. Most of the wooden strips of the boat were damaged and while moving on the boat's entire skeleton moved up and down. The boat was already half sunk. Food and water was in very short supply. The stoves were catching on fire and we put them into the sea. After that we ate raw food. We even lost the direction. It was really a miracle when we reached Ashmore Island.

Ken Arkwright ... His Story

by Karen Motta, aged 12

Mr Arkwright is sitting beside me, retelling his life story. He speaks confidently, has an incredible amount of knowledge and has obviously told his story before to other inquisitive journalists and students. He is a successful married man with two children and he lives in a large apartment overlooking the Swan River.

However, life was not always this easy.

I was born on the 16th of April 1929 to Rudolf and Frida Aufrichtig in Breslau, Germany (now called Wroclaw). I had a pleasant childhood, living in a thirteen room apartment with a number of servants and maids. I went to kindergarten in Germany and always had a lot of friends. I was only four years old when Adolf Hitler came to power in 1933.

One of the first things that Hitler did in 1934 was to shut down all Jewish businesses. My father ended up building roads, which was the fate of many Jewish businessmen.

In 1935 Hitler passed a law which prohibited Jews and non-Jews from mixing. My current school was in a Jewish community in the city of Breslau. Life became tough for Jews, especially the children who lost their childhood. They spent their early years looking over their shoulders. Trying not to stand out – that could cost a life.

I remember a Jewish school friend of mine who went to buy

an ice cream in a shop which had 'No Jews' written on the front. He disappeared and after a few days his parents were called to come and collect his ashes from the Gestapo. He had been arrested and had died in prison. Life took on new dimensions.

On November 1938 Kristallnacht occurred. Twenty thousand Jewish men were picked up off the street and sent to concentration camps. It was only temporary, they came out with instructions to leave Germany. All Jewish property was confiscated, every Jewish organization and every Jew was penniless. On that same night every Jewish Synagogue in Germany was either burnt or vandalised and every remaining Jewish business destroyed.

In 1939 when the war started we were gradually placed in ghettos. We moved from our spacious family apartment and lived in around sixteen different houses until we settled into a five room apartment. In each room lived one family. The whole house, the whole street, even the whole block was only Jewish.

Also in 1939 Hitler invaded Poland. If the Polish Jews got in the way of the German Army they shot them down.

Whatever happened to Jews before 1939 was immoral but not illegal since the necessary laws had been passed.

In 1942 schooling was prohibited for Jews. The children were locked up in a large Jewish cemetery from morning to night because our parents were already in forced labour. While we were there we cleaned up the cemetery and it actually began to look very nice. One day we got truckloads of paper bags with feet sticking out. These were Polish Jews who had not been shot or gassed but worked to death. Most of the bags didn't have names so we just buried them nameless. It was a foretaste of what was to come.

It wasn't long before I too was drafted into forced labour.

Before 1933 the Jewish community of Breslau had around twenty seven thousand Jews. Those who were still in Breslau in 1942 were just picked up off the street and deported. The first transport was of around thirteen hundred Jews. They had to dig their own graves when they got to Kaunas in Lithuania and then were shot. That was an ongoing process. Because my father had served for Germany in World War 1 we were deported fairly late. We were first sent to a labour camp.

When Hitler lost the Battle of Stalingrad he tried to build a trench from the Baltic to the Caucasus. It was meant to stop the Russian tanks from entering Germany. It was similar to Australia's rabbit proof fence. If you were Jewish or a POW then you dug from morning to night. When the tanks came I was moved to a concentration camp. We marched on foot for 400 km, around the same distance from Perth to Albany. It was a cold winter in November 1944 and quite a few people died. Then the Russians overran the camp and I escaped and lived underground under a false name, Klaus Shneider, until May 1945 when the war ended.

During my time in hiding I also visited a medieval city in the middle of Germany where I had friends who were pleased to see me. The city was still totally preserved, it had not yet been bombed. They gave me something to eat, dressed me and then there was an air raid. Around 80% of the city was destroyed in a few hours. I couldn't go to the air raid shelter because I would have been picked up by the Gestapo. I stood on the first floor of a building, only sixteen years old, watching the city die.

After that event most of the German citizens had no papers, no home and had lost some of their closest relatives. So the German Nazi Administration put some trains together and people queued up. They asked your name, your religion, your birthplace, where you lived and gave you a temporary Identification Card. They then told you to board the train. People had no idea where they were going. I was taken to a small city where I worked with non-Jewish peasants who did not know I was Jewish. At that time I was still with my father but had no idea where my mother was.

After the war I returned to Breslau and tried to find my

mother. By that time the city I had been born in had been taken away from Germany and given to Poland. Germany was divided and part of it was administered by France, Britain and America. The Russians looked after the rest. The Russian and Poles were not interested in getting me into Eastern Europe. So I had to walk from the place I had been liberated in to the border between the Western and Russian Zone of Germany. I walked and hitchhiked for around five months and was delayed slightly after I caught typhoid and was taken in by American troops. I went over the border (that was a river) in a canoe with the Americans and Russians shooting at me from both sides. From there I had to go to the Polish border. The Russians were taking furniture from Germany. They loaded it into trains and took it home. I hid in a cupboard on a freight truck. When they got moving I opened the door and the closet next to me opened too. There was another man who was doing the same. I only spoke German and I didn't know what he spoke. We didn't say one word to each other.

When I reached my home in Breslau I found my mother. It was then a Polish city so we moved on to Central Germany. I worked hard and achieved my German equivalent of a TEE. I also started studying medicine in Berlin. At that time Berlin was in the middle of a Russian zone. It was occupied by four different countries. There was a showdown in Berlin and the Americans and British had to supply the town by air with all the necessities like food and fuel. It was then that I decided to leave Eastern Europe. I had to leave Berlin illegally because no one, except the American troops, was allowed in and out.

I left Berlin with the help of the Americans. I was hiding under a soldier's coat, so that when the Russians looked in from the platform they would not see me. The Americans were quite happy to let me leave for Paris as it meant fewer mouths to feed. I travelled by myself and my mother and father came afterwards. I spent four months in Paris before I could get a ticket on a boat to get to Australia. The ship was a converted army ship and it was very crowded. At that time no one would accept German currency so my passage was paid for by a Jewish welfare society. They also gave me some money in Australia to help me, which I had to repay.

I arrived in Fremantle, Western Australia and was met by a cousin of my father who had immigrated to Perth in 1938 before the war started. He helped me obtain a permit to come to Western Australia.

When I arrived in Australia I wanted to continue my medical studies but the West Australian University would not recognise my medical studies or even my TEE. My first job was a postman. I knew every dog in Maylands personally. After that job I managed a retail store. At the same time I studied accounting, economics and management by correspondence. I later had a job as an accountant. At that time my English was not particularly good. I had already learnt French, Russian, Latin and Greek but neither those nor my German were of any help while learning English.

I have lived in Australia for around sixty years and in that time have been involved with the Jewish community. I met my wife Judith in 1957 when we were both singing in the Temple David Choir. Together we had two sons, Peter and Kevin.

I don't blame Germany for the way I was treated. It wasn't Germany's fault; it was the evil deeds of the Nazis of Germany. Most of the people who were a part of the treatment of Jews in World War II are either dead or the same age as me: they no longer have any power.'

When I asked if Ken considered Australia or Germany his home he had one answer.

'The world is my home.'

THE SWIRL OF MEMORIES

'Everyone was handing out roses and hugging us ... It seemed like the whole of Perth had come out with flowers just for us.'

A Truly Great Australian

by Jane Woodward, aged 16

Each sunrise brings with it hope for the future and a new beginning. Every person on earth craves the freedom that Australians take for granted. In the late 1970s a young Vietnamese man had a dream of finding freedom because the life he had come to know was intolerable. It didn't matter where it was, as long as it wasn't in Vietnam. What decisions must face people living in an oppressed society when their only option for liberty is far away from the family that they love? Khiem Nguyen confronted those decisions and when he made his daring escape, Vietnam's loss became Australia's gain.

When Khiem reflects upon his years in Vietnam after the country had been reunited under communist rule, he recognises that it was easier when his mind had closed the door to that past heart of darkness. In some respects he can still only vaguely see the contour of that door, as if looking through a veil of mist but in others it is as vivid as if he carried a photograph of it in his hand.

The second Indo-China war began when Khiem was six years old and lived with his family in the market town of Choilon, approximately six kilometres from Saigon. He didn't ever comprehend the devastation that was occurring in his country because his remarkable parents sheltered him and his siblings during the war. During the Tet Offensive, they made light of the mortar fire and turned hiding under the bed away from gunfire into a game. 'They told us nothing so we were not afraid,' he said. When he saw dead bodies littering the countryside he said, 'I was not worried. I thought they were asleep.' When Saigon fell in April 1975, Khiem was fifteen years old and much more aware of the evil that had descended upon his country.

How does one remember the face of evil? Khiem didn't understand until the fall of Saigon that the shape of society depends on the ethical nature of the individual as well as on a political system. It seemed as if the war and the resultant communist victory liberated everybody from society's rules and taboos, and unfortunately, allowed people's natural capacity for evil to dominate their existence and actions.

The communist regime attempted to suffocate the conquered South Vietnamese – they were treated like animals. Life savings kept in the South Vietnamese currency were lost, propaganda was broadcast over public address systems from six in the morning until late at night attempting to brainwash the people into believing in the communist ideals, and their national consciousness was becoming humiliated and suppressed. All young people were obliged to attend nightly meetings where they were barred from leaving once they had arrived. Their purpose was first to prevent dissident groups forming and secondly to indoctrinate the young people further. They became the state's slaves, required to work digging water trenches to the paddy fields in mine and bomb infested territory, and the schools were transformed from learning institutions to venues where the communists tried to transform the children into their image of equality and brotherhood. They could not be seen in groups of more than four because the perception was that they were rebels. The roots of the regime were solidly established in lies, fear, corruption and moral poverty. The lower level administrators extended the indignities to whatever level they saw fit. The communists thought Khiem should be a man at fifteen and they handed him a weapon, 'an

AK47, without any training,' and told him, 'just to pull on that button when he saw anyone on the street after midnight.' He was forced to conduct a curfew patrol in his own neighbourhood between midnight and six in the morning and shoot anyone who defied it. If he refused his mission, the repercussions were enormous. He unwillingly became a part-time communist conscript and was used for some unspeakable purposes that it is clear he would rather forget. He vividly remembers being utilised to force a family from their home because the bureaucracy thought the family was rich as they lived in a big house. 'They thought the rich were sucking the blood from the poor. But this family wasn't rich. He was a hard working taxi driver. I had to hold my gun and be on guard and watch them cry. I felt so dreadful. I didn't want to do this but I had no choice.'

The people lost their privacy. Their doors were open for the police to walk into their homes at any time and take things that they thought were trappings of wealth. Their food supplies became scarce and hunger and fear became synonymous with living. Khiem conformed with the system for two years but then began to avoid the nightly meetings by hiding with friends and lying as to his whereabouts. His actions made it difficult for his family, because the police came looking for him, but they supported him. He dreamt of freedom and escape and planned elaborate getaways with his friends. He didn't think of the risks involved, just of hope for a future in a free world.

His salvation came by the hand of the Fifth Uncle who had managed to save US dollars and gold during the war. His uncle organised for his family, Khiem's grandmother and one member of each of his brothers' families to leave the country. Khiem was the one chosen from his family. He pleaded with his father to take his younger sister and twelve-year-old brother with him and eventually they found the means. His father's words still ring in his ears, 'Make sure that you look after them.'

Three times they were told that it was time to leave, and

three times they said their tearful goodbyes to later learn that it was a trap. When the fourth occasion came, they didn't say proper goodbyes because they didn't think it would happen this time either. 'Later that made me feel so bad.' The plan was that Khiem's mother would tell the police that he had taken his younger siblings to the countryside to visit relatives. Excitement and anticipation had been elevated in the past, so on the fourth occasion Khiem was cool-headed and without expectation. The aura of calm, underscored by a pervading fear of detection, accompanied him. He also felt immense responsibility for the younger children.

They moved to a meeting point and the organisers arranged for them to hide on the high canvas cover of a transport vehicle that was moving materials to Ca Mau on the southern most peninsula of Vietnam. The top of the vehicle was crowded with people, (including twelve of Khiem's extended family) but Khiem managed to lift his head to catch glimpses of the passing country-side because, he said, 'I thought it might be the last time I saw my country. I have such clear memories of green.'

The trip to Ca Mau took about nine hours over poorly sur-faced roads. It was terrifying because there was always a danger of being caught. The penalty for escaping was imprisonment and the risk of being shot. The vehicle finally stopped and Khiem's bones ached from the reverberation of the rocky road through his body. He kept close to his young brother and sister and they were herded with a sense of panic and excitement onto another truck before being taken and deposited into the grounds of a temple. Corruption and bribery could only assure safety to a limited extent. For two long weeks they slept outside the temple, managing to purchase some food and water from people living nearby. Numerous times they were told that 'tonight is the night' but their hopes were continually frustrated. 'We had been talking to other people and they said that they had been waiting for three months so I was in despair that we could ever leave.'

At midnight on 14th April 1979 they were herded onto a truck and driven to a beach. They had to be deathly quiet because although police silence had been bought in one sector, it had not been in others. Khiem felt horrified when he saw that the boat was only about sixteen metres long and three metres wide and there were just so many people milling about hoping to get on it. He was gripped with fear when he saw that the petrol tank was a loosely attached forty-four gallon drum. 'I worried so much about how such a flimsy boat could carry us to safety out into the sea. It was only meant for use in the rivers.' Khiem hung onto his sister and brother, terrified that he might lose them in the crowd. Staccato voices permeated the air like gunfire. Names were being called. Would they be on the list? There was so much fear in the air. The police might come. Khiem had to be brave for them all. Khiem's sister's name was called and then he heard his own. 'Move onto the boat or you'll lose your place,' they were ordered. The sense of fear and urgency gripped Khiem so badly that he could hardly breathe. His little brother's name was not called. His father's words echoed through his head, 'look after them, look after them'. There was no choice – his brother's name would surely be called. Khiem and his sister got onto the boat and found their cramped sitting place on the deck.

When the boat commenced its journey Khiem still hadn't found his brother among the 162 people cramped onto the deck and in the hold. His grandmother and uncle's family had made it, together with one cousin from each family. There were some people who were very seasick and Khiem spent four days fanning people to cool them. After four days and nights and eight separate attacks by Thai pirates who boarded the boat carrying axes, knives and old handguns, they arrived at an island off Malaysia with barely the clothes they stood up in. They had lost all their possessions including Khiem's glasses but were fortunate that his sister was one of the few women who was not raped. As Khiem sat on that deck, having lost his homeland, his little brother and all his possessions, he clung to his sister and dreamt of liberty. 'I knew there were two choices, freedom or death so freedom was worth any cost.' He didn't cry because he didn't have the energy after four days without food and water.

They had to swim to the beach where they camped in an enclosed area in the open for four weeks, living on a staple diet of coconuts that had fallen from the trees. During the day they covered themselves with coconut palm leaves to protect themselves from the sun. Every morning when they woke they were soaked with moisture. They bathed in the sea and managed to get some water from a well dug by Malaysian soldiers camped nearby. They were brutally treated by the soldiers who struck them with sticks when they didn't follow commands that were given to them in Malay. Khiem said, 'we thought it was the Vietnamese Army and we had landed at the wrong place. All the girls had to pull their pants down and they said they were checking for arms but that wasn't true.'

After four weeks they were taken on a four-hour boat trip to a refugee camp at Palau Bidong, on the west coast of Malaysia. 52,000 refugees camped on that small island. Their family acquired a two-storey hut made from sticks that measured approximately three metres by three metres. They were luckier than most people. They slept on the rough floor with beds made from bark. Three-day ration packs were provided and they lived off curried beef, sardines and baked beans for eleven months. Water was scarce and had to be fought for until the family dug a well under their house. They bathed in the ocean, washing their clothes while they were still wearing them and allowing them to dry on their bodies. They had to use the forest for toileting. They had to cut down trees to get wood to light the fire for cooking. Life was very tough but Khiem and his sister were happy because they had begun their journey to freedom. They knew that eventually they would find a new home. Nothing could be as bad as the oppression in his homeland. The whole time however, he had a sick worrying feeling about the fate of his brother.

Khiem later found that his brother's name had not been on the list and he was apprehended by the police. He still lives in Vietnam.

It was a sad day when Khiem's grandmother died, unable to cope with the arduous journey and the conditions in the refugee camp. The day they buried their grandmother was the day they were interviewed about coming to Australia.

'My sister and I were the only two people out of 162 who were chosen to come to Australia. It was very difficult to get into Australia. Everyone who went before us had their papers marked 'REJECTED.' My sister did it for us because she spoke English well. She had the government official laughing,' Khiem said. They had been having English lessons in a church from two weeks after their arrival and had heard that they could listen to whatever music they wanted to and wear whatever they wanted in a 'wonderful country called Australia.'

Khiem and his sister arrived in Australia on 18th April 1980, a year to the day after they arrived in Malaysia. He was wearing the same clothes and underwear that he wore when he left Vietnam. They were flown directly to Canberra and were worried when they looked out of the plane thinking that they were being taken into the middle of the country because it was so open. They were taken to a government flat that had been furnished from St Vincent de Paul and Khiem thought that he was in heaven.

One night he woke after a nightmare and found that his pillow was soaked from tears. He had cried for the first time for his country, his lost brother and his family.

It took time to adjust but every step of the way was worth it. Khiem is now happily married with two beautiful daughters, owns his home and has been in full time employment from fourteen months after his arrival.

Khiem's story has changed my perception of refugees. How could such a gentle, hardworking and loving man have endured so much and still thank the world every day for his existence? I recognise now that behind every face there is a story to tell. Refugees have not only enriched our country but facilitated our recognition of the lucky country that we live in. A country that should open its doors to those who crave freedom.

Khiem Nguyen is a truly great Australian!

Denada's Story

by Rosa Brown, aged 12

This is a story about a person, a refugee named Denada, a story about her time in detention, a story about our friendship.

Denada left Albania and went to Kosova to flee the war and it was in Kosova where she met and married Mark. Mark had been taken by force to join the Kosova Liberation Army in 1999. For a year Denada did not hear from or see Mark. Then Mark managed to escape from the KLA and would have faced execution if he did not leave Kosova. So Mark and Denada left together and came to Australia. They arrived here on an airplane with fake passports and ID because they hadn't had time to obtain visas. When they left the plane they explained to the guards and thought that they would be helped, but instead they were taken to Villawood Immigration Detention Centre. They spent more than 400 days there. At the end of 2001, Denada and Mark were released and went to live with Denada's uncle in Adelaide.

In June 2001 when I was in year six and lived in Canberra I went to a rally for refugees with my mum. There were six speakers and I found each one of them interesting. One of the speakers was Marion Lé, a migration agent. I had no idea of the terrible conditions refugees were having to face in Australia. I was very moved by the speeches and thought that I would like to help by writing to a refugee. Refugees have already suffered in their home country, experiencing war and famine. They make a terrifying escape and then, when they think the journey is finally over having reached Australia, they are taken to an Immigration Detention Centre for an indefinite amount of time. So at the end of the rally, I approached Marion and told her I would like to be in touch with a refugee in a detention centre. She knew Denada, because she was her lawyer. I wrote to Denada straight away. Denada could already speak and write some English, and I noticed her English improve as we corresponded. I told her about my life and asked her questions about detention. At the time I knew almost nothing.

Denada told me about how sad she felt in detention. 'I pray to Jesus to make me free one day, out of this gaol, because this is not detention, detention is just a name; this is gaol.'

Denada told me that it was very bad in detention and that she cried everyday. This made me sad, and want to help her even more. Through our letters we became great friends

The first time I saw Villawood was an aerial shot on the TV news and I had an idea of where my friend was. But the feeling I got the first time we drove into Villawood was sickening. We drove down to see a double layer of wire fencing and razor wire at the top and bottom of the fences. We were escorted into the visiting area by the guards. We were not able to take a camera to have a photo of Denada and me together. We had to sit in the hot visiting area surrounded by razor wire and guards. It's hard understanding that my friend has spent more than a year of her life in there and that so many others have as well. That night I had nightmares and couldn't sleep. Often on the news I hear about refugees and detention centres and find it disturbing knowing that there are children behind bars.

Denada came to Australia for a better life but here she lost everything, she tells me. She lost her freedom, her identity, her family and friends, her birthplace and home. After being in detention for ten months Denada was starting to feel the strain. Her health was getting bad and she was losing weight, she even started taking depression tablets.

Denada told me that during the night guards would come into their rooms at random. Even after Denada left a sign on the door asking the guards to knock, they continued to enter without permission. There were musters at very early times of the morning where the detainees would have to get up for a head count.

When Denada was only ten, there were a lot of demonstrations against the communist regime in Albania. Denada's family felt the strain. Every day her parents would remind her and her brother and sister not to tell anyone that they prayed or made the sign of the cross. Her parents said that if they did this they would be in a lot of trouble and could be put in gaol for twenty-five years. They felt they were isolated from the world. During the upheavals against the communist regime there was a lot of disruption and often the schools were closed.

When she was about sixteen, war hit Albania. There were a lot of troubles and the government gave orders for people to stay inside. Bullets were fired into their apartment on the third floor, and they would lie on the floor twenty-four hours a day. So Denada went to Kosova for a safer life, but two years later war broke out again when Serbia began ethnic cleansing against the Albanian Kosovars.

Denada is an intelligent, enthusiastic, kind person, even while she was in detention. She organised the children in there to play games such as hide and seek. When she spoke to them after she left, they told her that they were too sad to play hide and seek any more because she was gone. She won the women's pool competition and is good at table tennis. She was school champion at long jump when she was about twelve. She is good at learning languages and can speak fluent Italian, Albanian and English. She taught herself Italian by watching Italian cartoons on TV in Albania. When she was in her teens, she edited the church magazine, and was on the radio once. She won a painting competition for young people called 'Vincent's Friend'.

Denada is now out of detention and doing a TAFE course and

has applied for university entrance. She was accepted into university but cannot go because she has to pay overseas fees that she cannot afford. Denada was interviewed by *Cosmopolitan* magazine and asked about her hopes for the future.

'Before I left Albania, I dreamt of studying, going out with friends and shopping – all the things girls do. But I was denied that freedom when I arrived at Villawood. I am taking one day at a time. Ultimately, I want to become a psychiatrist to help other people.'

My friendship with Denada has affected me a lot. I am now more interested in human rights and Denada's experience has made me more aware of how lucky I am. I often think about Denada and refugees, and it makes me angry that there are detention centres in Australia.

Denada now lives in Adelaide and gave me her permission to tell her story.

The Story of Jenny K

by Chloe Costas, aged 17

In the spring of 1939, the German government gave two demands to the Polish government: firstly, to return the area of Danzig to German control. Secondly, to give Germany a road and rail passage across the Polish Corridor, which had separated Germany from East Prussia since the end of the First World War. In return, the German government would promise to defend Poland against the Soviet Union. The Polish government refused. On the first of September that year, Poland was invaded by the German army. Jenny was eleven years old. Her father had gone to America just before the war started, and she had no brothers or sisters. She lived with her mother, in the small town of Krasnik, near the university city of Lublin where, she proudly tells me, the Pope studied. Jenny didn't officially become a refugee until the end of World War Two. However, her experiences in the lead-up to 1945 are the basis of her story.

After the initial fighting, which lasted a mere thirty-two days before the Polish government was forced to surrender, the Germans began to take over all aspects of Polish life. They settled Polish farms; the biggest and nicest houses in town were used to house military personnel. Police curfews were enforced.

'It was very scary, there was no food, because the factories, everything, they rip it, they take all the machines to Germany, because they needed bombs, so the people got no jobs.'

In addition, in November 1939 it was announced that Polish children were only allowed to attend school up to a grade four level. SS boss, Heinrich Himmler, said: *The sole goal of school should be: simple arithmetic up to 500; writing of one's name; a doctrine that it is a divine law to obey the Germans . . . I don't think that reading should be required.*

There is no doubt that the people of Poland understood this. Jenny recalls: 'We weren't allowed to go to school because the Germans didn't want to educate people . . .'

The Germans also realised the immense potential of the Polish, in terms of labour: by 1942, more than one million Poles had been deported to Germany to work as slaves, in farms, factories, mines and the like. These deportations were often very violent. For example, the Germans might drive into a community at night, burst into homes with weapons drawn, and order families into trucks to be taken away. While Jenny was not captured in this way, the method that the Germans used to deport her, along with her mother, was equally callous. One morning she and her mother caught the train from Krasnik to Lublin to do some shopping. Jenny had never been to Lublin before, so she was very excited. They got off the train in Lublin, had their tickets checked, and were directed to one side of the platform, while other people were directed to the opposite side. They had no idea what was going on until someone told them they had been caught by the Germans, 'like dogs in a street.' Prior to her capture, Jenny had heard stories of how others had been caught: 'They catch you in a street or in a church, when after the mass you come outside – and they take you.'

Despite the warnings of a local councillor to all young people to 'be prepared . . . to go to Germany,' Jenny and her mother were completely surprised and unprepared. Along with roughly two hundred others they were packed into trucks and taken to some barracks in Lublin. Jenny was fourteen.

Conditions in the barracks were terrible. Every day all the

prisoners were counted, but no names were taken. It was next to impossible to escape, due to the high fences and guards. There were three basic meals per day. Breakfast consisted of a mug of tea and bread, while lunch and dinner were both soup: 'We get . . . soup like the army, barley and big beans and five or six slices of bread, really brown bread.'

The barracks were quickly overrun with lice. Once a week the prisoners were marched in lines to the public baths where they could wash themselves. One night, after a month of this, everyone who had been captured was marched to the railway station, under guard, and bundled onto a train to Germany.

Once in Germany, the Poles were treated viciously. The German government's use of propaganda labelled them *untermenschen*, meaning 'sub-human.' They were forced to wear a purple 'P' on their clothes, much as Jews were forced to wear a Star of David. Jenny recalls: 'We got the number P, because we Polish people. Just in case the police catch you they knew it. If we don't have, we get maybe twenty belts.'

In the lead-up to the war, Hitler had made claims that the Germans living in Poland had been forced to live under an inferior people. Newspaper articles urged German citizens to treat the Polish as inferior.

Poles in Germany were segregated from the 'master race' of Germans. Jenny was not oblivious to such racism: 'I remember we walk in the street, and there were two German ladies, young ones, and they've got a little boy, two or three, and they walk and say "Heil Hitler," and then they saw the number, the P, and say "You schweine Pole" – we have to go across the road.'

The Polish deportees had to endure inhumane living conditions. Jenny, like labourers across Germany, worked a twelve-hour day. She got up at 5am every morning, started work at 6am, then at 6pm was sent back to the barracks where she slept, with twenty other female Polish slaves (including her mother). A further twenty male Polish slaves were housed in a separate barracks. They were all given forty minutes for lunch. During this twelve-hour day, Jenny and her fellow captives were made to help manufacture bombs. Jenny was given the hardest job: a fiddly task which required her to shave minuscule amounts off the parts, measuring each to the millimetre. Her boss, the factory owner, expected her to understand this difficult task straight away. She remembers that, 'in the beginning they didn't tell you that the shavings have to be separate . . . Like aluminium and some different stuff, I put together and the German boss come and hit me in the head. My head was going around. For three days I had headache. But nobody tell you nothing.'

This was enough to persuade Jenny not to attempt to sabotage the bomb parts: she was fully aware that if she did, she would be sent to a concentration camp. However, because she was so fast at completing her task, she was able to lighten her load some days. The German lady who had made them before the Poles arrived had managed to produce roughly sixty or seventy every day. Jenny found she was able to make from eighty to one hundred in the same amount of time.

'I was so quick, so I hiding some for next day.'

For this fifty-five hour week, the slaves were paid two marks. This was the price, roughly, of a dozen matches.

The repetitive nature of the work Jenny was forced to do caused huge blisters on her hands. A kind German lady at the factory spoke to Jenny about them:

'She told me, not only me but another girl, when we were bleeding, but we didn't have any cream, no fat, nothing, and she say "You know what? When you go to loo, just put the urine on, and they heal." So we did. It stung like vinegar, but after three days it was working. It was like silk hands.'

Despite this, physical reminders of the blisters did not disappear completely for ten years.

Slave labourers were given just enough food to ensure they could keep working. In the factory where she was taken to work,

Jenny was given three scant meals per day. Breakfast was a drink, similar to tea, but made from 'German herbs,' two slices of bread and half a slice of devon. Lunch consisted of one piece of bread (they were given five slices per day) and a bowl of soup: 'sweet turnips and cabbage, big pieces, and potatoes.' Dinner was the same, but with two slices of bread, and the other half of the devon.

Jenny remained at the factory until the end of the war – three years in total. These three years of captivity ended abruptly upon the defeat of Nazism in Europe. After spending two days and nights hiding in a cellar with nothing to eat but raw beetroot and carrots, the Poles emerged to find the factory compound virtually destroyed by American soldiers. Upon seeing the purple 'P', a Polish officer was immediately found to speak to them in their own language. He told them that the war was over, and they were free to go. They remained at some nearby barracks for two weeks, and then had to decide whether to return to Poland or try to make a new life somewhere else. With admirable foresight, Jenny's mother predicted that Stalin would be as bad as Hitler, and opted to remain in Germany. So, still together, they became refugees and were moved to a camp roughly twelve kilometres away. At the camp, a doctor told Jenny she would have lived only another six months had the war not ended. She was eighteen.

At the camp, she also met a 26-year-old pharmacist, who could speak English. Jenny's mum kept saying, 'You'd better get married, and be family, they is treated different, you know.' So Jenny got married.

Two years later she had her first son, and in 1949 the family of four (including Jenny's mother) moved to Australia. In 1953 they moved to a small town adjacent to the still developing national capital – Jenny's mum saying that Canberra's climate was similar to that of Poland. She has lived there ever since. She has worked in places like the Members' dining room at Parliament House (before new Parliament House was built), and has served many now famous politicians. Gough Whitlam apparently once told her she looked like the Queen. When Harold Holt was Prime Minister she would take him his breakfast in his office, and once, she tells me with a cheeky smile, she sat down in his chair.

After her first husband died, Jenny remarried, and had a second son. He and his brother both live nearby, and she now has two primary-school aged grandsons, on whom she dotes. For a woman who underwent such a traumatic experience, Jenny is remarkably cheerful and optimistic. She has returned to Poland three times since being forcibly removed in 1942, and hopes to go again soon. Jenny has been a captive, a slave and a refugee; a wife, a mother and a grandmother; a housekeeper, a waitress and, above all, a survivor.

For the Love of a Child: Mai's Story

by Khazmira Florentyna Bashah, aged 12

It was 14th February 1982, our aeroplane touched down at Perth Airport. Everyone was handing out roses and hugging us. It felt wonderful. It seemed like the whole of Perth had come out with flowers just for us. Many years later I was to learn that it was Valentine's Day.

Now, on 14th June 2002, here I was, waiting for a twelve-year-old girl to come and interview me about being a refugee. I was filled with so many emotions, as I had never in all these years been asked my story. I wondered what she would ask me and if I would remember how things really were in the Saigon we had fled. As I sat waiting for her to arrive, my mind drifted back to those years and many painful memories came back to me. My own memories and those through the eyes of my mother . . .

It was 1975 and the streets of Saigon were filled with beggars, food stalls, cyclos (motor bikes) and the usual throng of people. There were many smells of food and the heat made everything feel so very steamy. Rumours abounded about Vietnam going to war, about the Americans taking over the cities, and the threat of Communism was hanging over everyone.

My father was an army captain, my mother a nurse and they enjoyed a pleasant middle class way of life until 30th April 1975 when their whole world changed. War came with a sudden awakening for my parents; the Communist party came into power. My father was immediately put in prison. My mother, who was pregnant with me, was taken in the middle of the night every night to be questioned about my father's activities, but she was kept alive because she was a nurse and they needed her skills to repair the many wounded flooding into the city.

Many people were re-zoned into the hills away from their families. They were sent away with nothing. Many people took their own lives.

When my mother gave birth to me, she named me Mai. Before she had time to recover from the birth, she was told she would be going to Cambodia to nurse the soldiers. This was not a choice.

Mother was alone and knew she would have to go but if she took me I would surely die. She had befriended the nuns at a convent and as she handed me over to them she made a promise to herself that no matter what she would survive and come back for me. She was determined that we would be reunited as a family one day. She was determined to live.

My mother's days and nights in Cambodia were filled with terror. Her nursing skills stood aside as she became more like a butcher, sawing arms and legs off the wounded soldiers because there was no other way to treat them. So much pain, so much suffering was endured by so many.

The torture and cruelty continued every minute of the day. The only thing that kept my mother alive was the promise to come back for me when all this was over.

My mother was a good woman and the doctors she worked with felt she had much courage and a very strong will. She was determined that she would find me one day. The doctors formed a plan to help my mother leave Cambodia and be reunited with me. They signed papers saying she had gone mad and that she should be released. The Viet Cong almost had a fear of the insane: they were the only people in the country to be left alone. They decided to release my mother.

The doctors who had made this possible then disclosed to her that throughout the war they had gathered the names and addresses of many of the wounded they had treated. They tucked notes into my mother's clothing. She was to try to deliver as many notes as she could to the families of the wounded and dying.

Upon her return to Saigon my mother kept her promise and delivered the messages to the grateful families who for the first time in many months had news of their loved ones.

My mother and I were reunited in 1978. I was two years old. My mother knew then that we would have to escape. If we remained I would never have an education and I would never have a future. In order to survive we had to go. My mother continued with her pretence of being a mad woman and most of the time was left alone. We continued to struggle for food; all the while my mother looked for ways for us to leave Vietnam.

My mother did find someone who would take us and many other families in a boat to safety. We left our house in the middle of the night. We had not told anyone of our plan. So many of us were waiting on the shore to get on the boat to freedom. Suddenly flashlights, soldiers and dogs came out of nowhere. The fate ahead was inevitable. As we were all huddled into a shed to wait, a young soldier came up to my mother and scolded her for putting my life at risk. My mother told him of her hopes, dreams and aspirations for me. He took pity on her and said he would help her to escape back to Saigon instead of us being put to death. The young officer would distract the rest of the soldiers, my mother and I were to run and hide under the bridge until he came for us.

The plan worked but it seemed like we waited for hours under the bridge before he came and yelled at us to run as fast as we could. We heard the sounds of dogs and gunfire as we ran and ran. We ran through thick jungle and then my mother dropped to the ground and could not run any more. The young soldier carried my mother and me on his back to the safety of his own mother's house. We were given food and warmth and then had to make our way back to our house in Saigon. We unlocked the door and returned as if nothing had happened. The young hero had saved our lives.

My father was eventually released from prison in 1981. I was six years old. Things in Vietnam had gotten much worse and my father was determined that we all should leave. My parents said many times that they could die in Vietnam but this was not the way for me. I needed to go on and survive so that one day I could tell this story.

My father's uncle had a small boat and it was decided that we had to try once more to leave Vietnam. Twenty adults and thirty children travelled on the boat with us. We decided we would head for Malaysia as they were allowing refugees into their country. It was said to be a short journey of no more than two days. We had heard many frightening stories about the terror at sea. There were stories of pirates and cannibalism yet this almost seemed worth the risk as opposed to never having freedom again.

After six days we still had not reached Malaysia. We were lost at sea. We came across an oil rig and were given food, water and a new map to find our way to freedom.

When we arrived on the Malaysian shore we were told we had to sink our boat. As we were doing so and trying to get to shore, my father told me to hang tightly onto him. He jumped into the water and I let go. I fell straight to the bottom and almost drowned. Once again my parents' will to keep me alive made sure I was rescued and finally taken to the shores of Malaysia.

We remained in the camp for a month and were interviewed by American officials. We were asked if we wanted to settle in America but my father was very scared of them and said no. Everyone thought he was mad because now his application would go to the bottom of the list. The officials interviewing all the refugees were due to fly out over the Christmas period. A freak storm hit the island and they could not leave. The interviewing process continued. This time my father was interviewed by the Australians and was desperate to have his application accepted . . .

There was a knock on the door. I was startled and wondered where I was. My memories had taken me back to Saigon. A young girl in school uniform stood at the door. She was here for the interview and I knew I was ready to tell her our story.

Note

Mai Nguyen commenced school in Perth, Western Australia at Infant Jesus. She went on to Chisholm College and University. She gained a degree in Sociology, a Diploma in Adult Education and a Masters Degree. Today she works as a dedicated Community Settlement Services Worker assisting Vietnamese people settle into Australian life. She is currently campaigning for bilingual teachers. Mai believes the most important thing that can tie us together is a common language; it builds the bridges and differences between us all.

Mai's mother and father own a restaurant. Her father has never been back to Vietnam; he has not forgotten the price he has had to pay for leaving his many family members behind.

Mai's hopes for Vietnam are for freedom.

I will never forget the words Mai said to me: 'A person who becomes a refugee does not always come with the hope of a better life, they come for survival, because they cannot continue to live and be alive in the country they are fleeing from. It takes desperate steps to leave in small boats to set off for a place that may never let you stay, but none of that matters because you leave your country for Freedom!'

The Life of Sadie Wagner

by Jack Lander, aged 12

I first met Sadie Wagner about six months ago when she visited our home. Sadie is a German lady who fled from her country towards the end of World War Two. During our time together we talked about the hardship she had experienced through her life.

Sadie grew up in a small town on the outskirts of East Berlin. She lived there with her mother, father and older sister. She lived a very quiet childhood, as her parents did not have much money. When she was about seventeen World War Two broke out and Sadie's father had left the family home to fight the war in Russia. Life became even harder for Sadie and her mother and sister as food became very hard to obtain. They survived by growing their own fruit and vegetables and rearing chickens for eating and eggs. Meat was rarely available as the country's meat supplies were taken by the invading Russian armies. The family also survived by the mother giving decorated cakes in return for other household products.

It came to the time when the Russians came in and took over their town. They were not allowed to leave and became prisoners to the Russians. All remaining older men in the town were taken from their homes and placed in prisoner of war camps a long way away from their homes. The younger men of the town were left to work for the Russians. If they refused to do what they were told they were severely tortured and then finally shot. Sadie, as did many of the other young girls, saw many acts of cruelty. For example, one young man who refused to do what he was told was nailed to the table by his tongue and, when he couldn't hold his head up any longer, he was shot in the head. The women and young girls remained in the town to serve and look after the Russian armies.

The events over the coming months were to change Sadie's outlook on life forever. Sadie had been told of the many terrible things that had been happening in the town due to the Russians. Sadie was of very slim build and therefore decided to dress and act like a young man so she would not become a victim of the enemy's bad treatment. For many months Sadie worked for the Russians alongside other young German men, doing as she was told, and not being found out that she was really a young woman. During this time Sadie saw many horrible things, from young German men hanging in doorways with parts of their bodies missing, to young men being shot in the head in front of her for not answering a Russian soldier in a correct manner. It was on one of these occasions that Sadie, forgetting who she was, screamed when a young German fell down dead at her feet after being shot in the head. Instantly, Sadie was surrounded by a group of Russian soldiers. The one closest to her proceeded to rip her beret from her head, causing her hair to fall down to her shoulders. Straight away Sadie's hands were tied behind her back and she was dragged out of the hall where she had been working, loaded into a waiting truck with eight soldiers surrounding her and taken back to her home. Sadie was dragged out of the truck and into her home where her mother tried to run to help her. Sadie's mother was knocked to the floor and held there while Sadie was thrown down onto a nearby lounge. She was raped brutally by each and every one of the eight soldiers, while her mother cried helplessly, unable to help her daughter. The soldiers just laughed and shouted abuse at Sadie and her mother. After the soldiers left Sadie's mother bathed and dressed Sadie's cuts and abrasions.

From that time until the Russians left the town, quite often soldiers would call at Sadie's home for food and other services. It became a regular occurrence.

Sadie's whole life had been turned upside down, not able to trust or get close to anyone.

Many months passed and, finally, the Russian armies left the town. Sadie's mother had not heard from her husband for months, not knowing if he was dead or alive.

Gradually, Sadie tried to get her life back into order. She loved to dance, so Sadie started to go dancing on a Friday night at the local church hall. There, Sadie met an older man, fifteen years older than her. His name was Robert and he had heard about all the things that had happened to Sadie and her family. Sadie became quite close to Robert over the next few months as he was very patient and understanding and was very protective of Sadie.

Some time passed and Robert asked Sadie to marry him and follow him to Australia where he had been given a job opportunity. Sadie and Robert were quickly married and lived with Robert's mother, who did not like Sadie. She did not think that Sadie was good enough for her son because of what had happened to Sadie in the past. Robert's mother made life very unpleasant for Sadie, especially after Robert had left for Australia to start his new job. Sadie had to stay with her mother-in-law for twelve months before Robert had enough money to bring Sadie out to Australia.

When she arrived in Australia, Sadie lived in a migrant hostel with other German migrants. She slept in what was like a big dormitory containing twenty-four beds with very basic bed coverings. Sadie lived there for a further six months without her husband until he had enough money to put a deposit on a small house where they would live their entire married life.

Robert and Sadie had one son. They worked very hard to achieve the things they needed to make life comfortable for their small family.

Sadie's father never came back from the war, so it was presumed that he was killed in the war. Her sister became mentally ill due to what had happened to her during the war and was found hanging in the bathroom when she was twenty-five years old. Sadie never saw her mother again, but kept in contact with her until she died alone in their family home ten years ago.

Sadie has lived a very quiet life with her husband and son, until Robert died suddenly eight years ago. Since then, Sadie has lived comfortably, but lonely, in their home. She has many good friends who care for and look after her, and a loving son who makes sure that Sadie has everything she needs in her old age.

I WATCH THE WORLD AROUND ME CHANGE

'We need these stories to give human faces, not numbers, to the refugees who arrive on our shores.'

The Refugee Story

by Pharan Akhtarkhavari, aged 13

There are different types of prejudice in the world: prejudice of country, colour, language and worst of all prejudice of religion. Throughout the history of the world, many people have suffered persecution because of one or more types of prejudice. In the 21st century we are still witnessing persecution and prejudice.

The refugee story I have chosen is about my uncle and his family, who suffered because of religious persecution. Even though this is my uncle and his family's story, it is the typical story for any refugee.

My uncle came to Australia in November 1991 as a religious refugee from Iran. He is a member of the Baha'i Faith. Many Baha'is from Iran were forced to seek refuge throughout the world after the Islamic revolution, which occurred from 1978 to 1979 in Iran. Since the revolution in Iran, Baha'is in Iran have not had clear futures.

He told me there was no security of life or of even having a life, and absolutely no freedom. He said they wouldn't even let you go to university; they would exclude you from receiving a tertiary education. Baha'is in Iran suffered a lot for no apparent reason. As a Baha'i, I know we want peace for the whole world, not for it to be a divided race. We believe in respect for all other religions and tolerance to others. Baha'is weren't even allowed to go to work or have a job. They were considered second-class citizens.

My uncle's plan was to escape from Iran just to have some freedom. He wanted to be counted as a citizen, not a second-class citizen. He wanted his children to have an education. He wanted to become a civil engineer but he couldn't if he stayed in Iran. So my uncle and his family escaped to Turkey. My uncle wanted the United Nations to choose a good country for him and his family to live in for the rest of their lives. My uncle told the United Nations that he already had his sister in Australia for a support network and that it would be helpful to go there, but he said it was their decision. The United Nations sent them to the Australian embassy in Turkey to talk to the ambassador to explain their situation. After the United Nations, the embassy and my uncle had all talked, they decided to accept my uncle and his family for refugee status in Australia. So they came to Australia and moved to Toowoomba in Queensland where my mum and dad were living at the time. In the end my uncle was really pleased because they are all safe and happy now.

Now I will go into detail of the escape out of Iran. First my uncle and the family caught a bus to Tabriz from Shiraz which is approximately a two day drive. Then in Tabriz they got a car from friends and went to Makou down the back streets, which weren't very busy and didn't have soldiers checking identification (Makou is the border town of Iran and Turkey). Then from Makou they walked for seven days and nights, until they got to a village in the mountains. Then from this village they drove to Ankara, which is the capital city of Turkey. They stayed in Ankara for two months. The family then went and stayed in Neede for fouteen months. They then got great news of being accepted as refugees in Australia. They came to Australia all excited to be free of all the religious prejudice of the past. This part of his life my uncle said, was very distressing and scary because they didn't want to get caught, they just wanted to be free and not counted as second-class citizens.

My uncle and his family adjusted very well here in Australia.

At first it was a struggle because they had no transport, no house and almost no life. The only person and family they had were my mum and dad. My uncle and aunty had to learn English very quickly because they wanted to succeed at university. Each of them had to work very hard at university. They both got distinctions and high distinctions in their subjects.

When they got here they were so surprised that everyone was treating them so fairly. Now twelve years have passed and my uncle is a main roads civil engineer, my aunty is a registered nurse and my two cousins are in their senior years in high school and doing great and achieving high marks. My family has worked very hard to get where they are today. They are extremely happy that they made the decision to leave their troubled life in Iran and start a new life in Australia.

I hope after reading this story about my uncle and his family that you know what refugees go through to get to our great country. This is just one of the gripping stories about someone coming from a Middle Eastern country to seek freedom in Australia.

To Hell and Back

by Aidan Fawkes, aged 15

A once free flowing river in the centre of Halabja, the world's 'most beautiful' city, has dried up, the land around it devastated. Piles of dirt create a sultry atmosphere in and around the Iraqi region of Kurdistan. Buildings have crashed to the earth, homes ripped apart. War has destroyed a once exquisite city, forcing many to flee their home country and their way of life. This is what happened to Pishtiwan and his family. This is his story.

Pishtiwan was born in 1984 in Iraq, the second child in his family. Soon after his birth, the family fled to neighbouring country Iran, leaving his whole life – memories, family and home behind. His father took what he could, however it wasn't much to take from a country which had been his home all his life. War was approaching and survival was getting harder and harder by the day. On one occasion, Pishtiwan and his family were having lunch. Suddenly and unexpectedly a missile landed in their front yard. They then knew it was time to flee the country.

The first few months in Iran were tense. The family was still on the run. They were still illegal emigrants in the minds of the Iraqi officials, as they had left the country without telling the government. They didn't have a place to hide. For five years, Iran was home for the family. Pishtiwan and his brother attended school and his father had a well-paying job. Life was stable for them.

In 1989 after a long war with Iraq, Iran was a devastated

country, and the government was forcing refugees out of the country. This caused dismay and insecurity for Pishtiwan and his family, as again they had to move to another country.

'All around you Pakistani border control personnel eyeing you up, trying to find a flaw in you, suspecting you for everything. Try to look away, but remain aware of your surrounds. Men with guns in every direction. One wrong foot and death would be a prospect. Stay close, keep moving forward. Remain unnoticed . . .'

Pishtiwan and his family were able to make it past the border with caution. Not saying anything, not acting differently. His father had earned some money that secured his family a pass into Pakistan.

'A lot of smuggling goes on between Afghanistan and Pakistan. There are many people who are suspect at the border and everyone is treated as a criminal. It is very dangerous and very scary. At any one moment, a guard could turn on you and send you back in the direction you came from – and no one would dispute him. It was one of the scariest times in my life,' Pishtiwan said.

From the border, Pishtiwan, his father and his brother made it to Quetta, a very hot and dry city in western Pakistan. They stayed here for eleven years, having to be cautious and alert at all times. Pishtiwan fitted in well, looking like the locals and speaking their language. His appearance made him the member of the family to head onto the streets and purchase food and other goods needed for the family's wellbeing.

Pishtiwan's father however had problems fitting in with the culture, and it was hard for him to roam the city without being picked up by the police. After returning from a day out with a feast for his family and friends to celebrate Ramadan, Pishtiwan's father was arrested and taken to the police station. He had done nothing wrong, and the injustice that occurred shows the levels of respect to people from ethnic backgrounds shown in Pakistan.

He was asked to give up money and the groceries he had bought. He didn't comply with the policeman's request and was put in gaol for twenty-two days, fifteen of those spent in hospital. It was up to the United Nations, who had granted Pishtiwan and his family refugee status in Pakistan, to have him released from gaol.

'Pakistan is a country with many different cultures. There is a lot of racism in Pakistan because of this,' Pishtiwan said.

In 1992 they moved to Islamabad, the capital of Pakistan and were granted a benefit of 3500 rupees a month ($A100). There they applied to migrate to one of the four countries that were taking in refugees – USA, Australia, New Zealand and Finland. The UN prepared their application, which was rejected by the USA, on the basis that Pishtiwan's father was unable to work, as he couldn't speak English. They then tried for New Zealand and eventually received permission to migrate to Australia. Pishtiwan's mother was upset about the whole idea of leaving her home, and refused to migrate. She remained in Pakistan, intending to head back to Iran. This is a sensitive issue to Pishtiwan even today.

Iraq is still a dangerous place. There is an 80 per cent chance of death upon return to Pishtiwan's native country. However he says he would like to return home one day and meet up with his surviving relatives.

'There is only one way to get into Iraq today. That is to travel to Syria first and create a fake Iraqi passport there,' Pishtiwan said.

His family is safe now and Pishtiwan is extremely happy in Australia. He has many friends at his high school. Pishtiwan is doing well. His goal is to pass VCE and become a medical scientist. He wanted to become a pilot, however he says no Middle Eastern person is trusted to become a pilot after September 11. He can speak seven different languages and his future is heading in the right direction.

Zina's Story

by Zina Romanov, aged 19

Ten years ago, in a small town named Vinnista, in the country now called Ukraine, lived a family, my family.

The picture is directed at a four-year-old girl, one girl who was not suffering, living perfectly in the 1980s away from any wars and troubles. This four-year-old is me, and I did not know what really went on behind my back and how hard the ones who loved me were fighting. The war went on behind closed doors.

As we all know most of us do not learn from history's mistakes. I am a Jew, and many would say that being a Jew is not an advantage. Actually many people would say that it is a defect, a fault. In Russia, to my horror, I have to admit it is so. Well the people in my neighbourhood had such thoughts, but it was not until I was six that I was told how bad it was being Jewish. There was an incident that made me realise this. It happened very quickly and went unnoticed by many, yet it affected me and a lot of my friendships.

A women in a high rise next to my house decided that she had had enough of the small, chubby six-year-old running around in the playground with her friends. She came out and concentrated her look on me. She watched us play for a while and then she yelled, 'You are a Jew, you do not belong here!' It echoed all around the street and people looked at me and then at her. The silence was unbearable. It sounded very stupid, but from that moment on I knew I was different. It is this feeling that singles you out of a group of people. Thinking about it now I still have the same feeling. I am definitely older and I understand that what it means is perfectly normal. At that time my parents did not want to bother me with the information and the truth I was entitled to know. They wanted to protect me. And it was this sense of security that they kept for so long that hurt me in the end. I found it harder to blend in with people for the rest of my time spent in Russia.

This incident happened back in 1989. At the beginning of the year 1990 we arrived in Jerusalem, Israel. Once again I was not told the reason for abandoning my dear friends who had been a part of me, lives engraved into me forever. 'I am being taken to a better place,' I told my friends, nearly crying. As the bus drew further and further away something dawned upon me. I did not know what it was then but I know what it is now. A sense of understanding, knowing beforehand, that nothing is as easy as you want it to be.

Our trip to Israel was not something I can recall with happiness. People got mugged in broad daylight, police were bribed into letting people pass. I saw this and yet never understood why it was happening. Our baggage got ripped, the men of the family physically abused. And the shock of my mother nearly being taken away is something that will live with me for the rest of my life.

Israel was not what I expected. Not the promised land. I grew used to it and its demands as well as tragedies. You had to blend in. I learnt the language and obtained friends. It was easier with friendships as most of the people living in Israel were Jewish but Israel had its own problems and bad habits. The main problem at that time was the Gulf War, when Iraq launched missiles at its neighbours including Israel. My school consisted of 75 per cent Jewish students and 25 per cent Arab students. And every day I was reminded that one of these children might place a bomb or light a fire or worse.

Within two months of our arrival we were hiding in shelters and carrying gas masks everywhere. In that period people did not live, people lost their hope, they feared death as it was so close. Innocent lives were taken, young soldiers killed for nothing. Many Russian immigrants lost their children in this war, some we knew, some we did not. As usual I did not understand what was happening. By that time my name had changed to Ilana. With my name I stayed the same, very naive as I think back to it. I wish now I had understood how hard it was for my parents. For everyone. In a way I feel selfish not having known. They had to work and look after my grandparents and me. Everyday they feared. It is horrid when I think back to those moments. I have never actually talked about the war to anyone. I heard myself saying 'They would not understand'. When we heard 'nachash tzefa' it was the first warning, telling us the bombs were being thrown at us, and we either went into hiding or came back out. This was the national sign for the coming of the nachash (snake) or its departure. The gas masks – what were they for? I would ask. I can still remember its rubber smell and its horrible elastics that came over your head and made it hard to breathe. Also the big filter at the front.

I would sit in the corner of the room wondering if the roof would cave in, or would a bomb land in the middle of the tiny room, would we all be killed? At that time I hated the fact that we had come to Israel. I sit and think back – I did not learn to love Israel as many people do. I am always criticised for this. Whether this land is the promised land or not it took so many lives to keep it the 'promised' land. Why is that so? People tend to forget the hard times a country has faced and also the young souls who were lost. I can never make a decision about my true feelings towards Israel as it never came to be my home. It is a country my cousin has to defend – my only wish is to be there to defend him.

After the war my father set out on a journey to find a country where his daughter would have a right to choose whether she wanted to join an army or not. There is a rule or, rather, an imposed obligation in Israel that once you are a citizen you must go to the army as soon as you turn eighteen.

My father's journey was long and he experienced many dead ends. When he arrived in Australia he wrote to us, telling us how wonderful it was. He also wrote that this country had a lot to do with freedom of choice, great opportunities, and that there was a large number of Jews. I feared the move. I was ten years of age by that time and had grown a bit. I required some knowledge and a move did not seem the best alternative. We were also going away without my grandparents with whom I had spent most of my life.

The trip was very traumatic for my mother and me. We came here, again not knowing the language and not being able to communicate. I found Australia to be easy going, laid back and a place I could easily blend into without extra trouble. It is here that my true personality blossomed. I finally understood the meaning of life. Weird as it may sound, I now know what I want to do with the rest of my life whether it be happy or sad, in one place or another. And yet I still do not think of Australia as the country that I can call home.

I never want to move again, as moving is the breakage of all bonds, all that is so firmly rooted to the ground. But in the future I would like to go back to Russia, Ukraine and Israel but I do not think I could live in any of those countries again.

My families are there but they may have forgotten me. Besides these people, I have nothing there, except my childish memories and the happiness that I thought once existed.

1112: Anhar – Iran to Woomera

by Hannah Moore, aged 16

I Am Here With Hundreds Of Hopes

I am sitting here waiting for sunrise, my screams do not reach anyone. It feels as if I am screaming underwater.

I am sitting here hoping for golden dreams, but the thief of the night has robbed these very dreams away from me.

I am an injured bird that wants to talk to everyone, but others think of me as deaf and dumb.

I am alive without oxygen, I am suffocating to be freed. I am a stranger in this place, but can see the accidental fall from the cliff on the horizon.

I wish to escape from this cruel razor wire, I wish to escape from loneliness in captivity.

I am struggling to be freed, I am struggling to grab the pearls that are released from the eye of the night. I long to see the rainbow in the morning sunlight.

When will the light appear?

By Anhar (a translation)

'I don't know,' I whispered.

'But Hannah, why do you think I am in here, when will I get out? I just want to know what you think.'

There was another long pause, then, 'I don't know, soon I hope.'

I did hope, but it wasn't what I thought. I thought months, many months, maybe a year or maybe never. Anhar was braver. She measured the time in weeks, she even counted days. I gave her a watch and she watched each second tick by. Her memory is her life now, each second now reminds her of how things used to be and her present is blurred by her past. She remembers . . .

~

My mother's long and pointed fingers placed each object on the table with a certain gracefulness. The glass bowls that hung on the wall every other day of the year were now full with over-flowing fruit. The traditional candle was centred between the six other gifts of the New Year. I watched as she smoothed the white tablecloth of invisible creases and I sat in awe of her beauty. The light touched her face – my dad always noticed. My brother Bayan, only sixteen then, would come in, and then Dad. Year after year, I watched her set the table.

Now her tired hands place the makeshift bowls on the floor of our donga. Her loose wrists seem to forget their work, resting every few moments on her wrinkled forehead. The nails on her fingers are brittle and her skin tired beyond its years. Her deep eyes mourn the loss of another life. I watch her thoughts drift back to Iran where she would prepare the New Year's table. She dares not compare her old life to the new; it scares all of us to remember.

I remember . . .

Bayan walked into the house, his face quivered as he moved his hand to expose a deep cut on the tip of his ear. Dry blood streaked his cheek and tissue stuck to the open cut. He swallowed hard as he told how the boys at his school drew a knife and cut him, how they laughed. He looked down as he told how no one would bandage his ear, how nobody cared. He didn't cry but blinked back a glimpse of the desperation I recognised in his eyes. He walked away alone because I couldn't comfort him with the hope of a better day. We all knew the worst was yet to come.

We sit here avoiding each other's tired eyes and our limp but truthful bodies. In silence Bayan begins to move from the floor. He walks idly out of the room. Mum follows soon after forgetting the importance of the setting – of this New Year ritual. I am left with my father in this room, just another detainee.

I am one of many, I am number 1112. Bayan is 1113 and my friend Firoozeh is number 159. You can roughly guess the number of months a person has been in here from their number. Firoozeh has been here almost twenty-six months, over two years. I laugh at the mockery of the watch I wear, how each second ticks by slowly, carefully measuring the seconds, the minutes, tiny parts of the months and years. It has been 472 days. I vividly remember the first. It was confusion, since then it has been fear.

I remember . . .

My teacher shoved the heavy book in my hand. It smelt old and tired. The pages were limp with age, each corner soft with the fingers that had touched it. It was beautiful, carefully written and decorated. Tightly bound with leather and titled in fancy gold print. Qur'an. I dared not protest the attempt to convert me – Mandaeans didn't have that right. I prayed silently, in my own Mandaic language. I imagined the writings of the prophet Yehya bi Zekaria, John the Baptist, and I found strength to bear my teacher's merciless words. I only walked the streets of Ahwaz now with my father or my brother. A Muslim man could always tell a Mandaean. I hid behind my father's thin body, always on the inside of the footpath. I walked quickly and directly and I spoke of my religion to nobody. Everyone in Iran tried tirelessly and aggressively to make me believe in Allah. It was always Allah they talked of. It would please Allah if I were taken from my family to become a Muslim. It would please Allah that I was so unhappy and so afraid.

I remember . . .

I stumbled over a rise in the footpath and felt the dampness touch my leg. I knew it was dangerous, I'd seen other Mandaeans being attacked on the streets before. I sensed it was acid, something powerful that wanted to hurt me. I grabbed my skirt and held it from my skin so it didn't burn. I kept running. I couldn't blink away the face of the man whose arm had reached out and thrown this at me. I caught a mere glance of him on his motorbike, but enough to see his eyes looking back at me in disgust as he rode into the thick of the traffic.

People watched, some shouting as I ran past them on the footpath, knocking their children or their shopping trolleys. I was only a Mandaean. I was lucky to leave with only a burnt *chador*.

'*Stop.*' Their accents are harsh and the hate with which they yell makes my stomach churn, '*Stop yelling ya little bitch. Sit like the rest of the people in here and wait. Next time I don't want to even hear ya voice, if you're going to yell, yell in Australian, ya friggin' dago.*'

The ACM guards are like that Pasdar who walk through the streets demanding respect of everyone, especially Mandaeans. The guards' batons hang like guns and their boots tread with the same power. Some are kind but it's hard to know whom you can trust.

I remember . . .

It was a lifetime ago that we left Iran. Time crept by as if giving us opportunity to reconsider our decision. Time stirred in the middle of the night and woke me into a sharp consciousness. I packed as instructed and followed my father to the car. It was only a short trip but one that seemed too long. Drawn out with a sense of fear, we arrived in Indonesia. We spent only two hours in total in the open, otherwise we stayed quiet and nervous in the hotel. My mother shot glances at my father. Her eyes began to sink into her face as she came to doubt our leaving. Bayan and I noticed but didn't say anything or let on that we knew. It was too delicate a situation to feed the doubts my parents already had.

I saw fear rise in my mother's chest, fear of realising her doubt. Fear that rose and fell from the side of the boat in thick bile from her mouth. There was a line of people on the side of the blue boat. Mothers held their children to their chests as their husbands watched helplessly. We ran out of water on the ninth of the eleven days we spent at sea. The weathered boat gave way to the ocean, cracking slightly through the centre. Young children bucketed the water with brave strength, avoiding their desperate parents who hung from the edge of the boat, resting their hands on the side, some with their hands on their head, some protecting their body while others shielded their eyes from what they saw of themselves being swept with the waves to somewhere far away.

What was swept away with the current hasn't returned. I sit and stare through the door of the donga. The sun falls into the red sand. My view of the sunset is fragmented, I only see slithers of it through the gaps in the fence. I listen to the ticking of my watch, how carefully it marks out each second, I watch the departing sun signal the end of the day and I listen to the changeover of guards.

Time keeps moving, slowly, carefully while I watch the world around me change and sit, silent, still, eyes only, just a number – 1112

~

'Hannah, these are just a few of our problems,' Anhar stated.

'I know,' I said. I didn't know at all. I couldn't begin to imagine real fear.

There was another pause.

Anhar stumbled over the broken English, 'Hannah, I had to leave, you know, I cannot go back.'

'You'll be out soon,' I whispered. I hoped, but it wasn't what I thought. I thought months, many months, maybe a year or maybe . . .

Hope to Survive

by Zana Mujezinovic, aged 17

We hadn't eaten for seven days since we were captured and that house in sight might have been a good sign of some food or at least water that hadn't been poisoned. We got off those buses. There were eleven of them full of women and children. As we followed the drivers and some of the men who waited there for us, I didn't know where to turn to any more. Those dark-dirty walls that made the house look dead and scary on one side and on the other side a wall with shining daylight pushing through tiny holes. The floor was covered with crushed glass. It seemed like it was telling us something, maybe something we all waited for. Better said, we didn't know what to wait for any more. Was it survival or death? The walls might have been telling us something but which side do we choose: the dark one or the other dark one with a little light that was like a sign of survival? Maybe in the end our destiny would be chosen by others and not by us.

In the house they put us all into one huge room. It was as huge as half a soccer field. It had no furniture except old mattresses in the corner which were ripped and full of blood marks. The window was hidden behind a dark curtain. The people in the room were terrified, tired, confused, hungry and God knows what else. Impatiently we waited for the next instruction. All of a sudden there was screaming, howling, you couldn't even understand what was happening. The next thing I saw was the young girls and boys (from the age of twelve) being put into the corner where the dead mattresses were. As a seven-year-old I just stood there questioning what was happening: why are they separating kids away from their mothers, why are they crying so much? But the questions didn't seem like they were going to be answered for me.

Suddenly my mum grabbed my brother and me and pulled us close as if someone was taking us away from her. My brother was the victim. A monster, so he looked to me, was pulling him away from us. 'He's only eleven, what do you need him for?' a loud voice above me shouted at the monster. In all that confusion I realised that we were pushed in a small group into a tiny room that looked more like a garage with a double door instead of a roller door. All you could see in that room were handbags thrown onto the ground, which was covered with blood marks.

There were three men standing, all in their army uniforms, armed from head to toe. The guy on the door captured my eyes as I realised where I was. He had a long beard running from his upper lip down to his chest. The worst thing that made me even more scared was seeing the blood dripping down his beard. Around his waist he had a gun, a knife, a baseball bat and other things a criminal would have.

One of them approached my mum. He was asking for all the money and gold she had. Her trembling hand reached into her pocket and pulled out everything she had to satisfy him, but no, it wasn't satisfactory, and he smacked her with a bat and asked for more. As she got into a disagreement, he said to the guy at the door to take my mum away, take all her clothes off, and if he found anything to slaughter her – but was slaughter the word or was there more to it? In that moment my brother and I started crying, begging him to leave our mum alone, but he couldn't care less about us, or maybe he would take us as well. As another group was pushed into the room, my mum was pushed on the side, giving her the opportunity to take the rest of the money and gold out of her pants. I don't know how she managed to approach him with the rest but she did and he replied, 'I knew you have more, there is no need to lie, Muslim b****.' Then he took his bat and smacked her again across the back. I don't know how she managed to stand on her feet, but she did. She grabbed my brother and me and dragged herself out of that house. The walls were made of bricks like every house in Bosnia. The floor was dirty with no carpets and on the side there were only packing crates. The whole house stank like there were dead bodies lying around. As we stepped out into the fresh air the guy that caught my eye hit my mum one more time and tried to threaten her. He grabbed me and yelled, 'where do you think you are going with those earrings in your ears?' As my mum pulled me towards her he grabbed my ear and all I could see was blood. The pain was stronger than when I had my ears first pierced. Outside there were two trucks waiting for us to be transported to another house about two hours drive away.

Despite all the humiliation my mother went through she maintains her dignity. She is a dignified woman. She is a strong woman but my brother and I made her even stronger. She knew she had to fight to be able to protect us and some day, with or without our father, provide a stable home. The strength she had I've never seen. Seven days without eating, giving me and my brother the last crumbs she found in her pockets, drinking poisoned water and being beaten and still she managed to stay straight on her feet. It was admirable.

That night we settled into a house that they provided for us. It was located in bush with many trees and uncut grass. It looked like a jungle, which I have only seen in cartoons. The house was built out of bricks but wasn't finished yet. There was nothing inside. The walls weren't even painted; you could feel the air coming through. We would have to sleep on the cold floor or on the little clothing we had taken with us. But unluckily my mum forgot the bag outside in the garden where we had spent the day, so we couldn't even sleep on our clothes. It was a warm sunny day: if only we lived in peace. But at least we met a nice guy. He showed us where to find clean water and he also told my mum a secret.

My mum asked a guy in the house to go get the bag from where she left it. He said I'll open the door and you can go get it, I'll come with you. That's when it clicked in my head and I started crying. My mum ran back to me to see what was wrong but I couldn't tell her because that guy was looking. I begged her to stay and not to worry about the bag but she was determined to get it. She started walking with that guy towards the door, when my aunty called her back and offered herself to go get the bag. She was an older lady in her sixties. As my mum came back she gave up thinking about the bag and realised that our lives were more important.

The house was full of women and children and since we were one of the last ones in, we had to sleep under the roof. It was very unsafe where we tried to fall asleep. We lay next to an open area, which looked down onto the first floor. Since the house wasn't finished it didn't have a fence on the stairs or that area where we slept. The noise of grenades and guns made it impossible for us to fall asleep because they were basically falling somewhere near us. You could feel them and sometimes it felt that bullets were knocking on the roof, which was right above our heads. I was lying there on the cold floor, covered by my mother's body, praying to God that one of those grenades or bullets wouldn't hit through the roof.

In the morning as I woke up the first thing I noticed was that my mum wasn't there. As we reached the door my mum entered. She hugged us both and whispered, 'lucky I didn't go out last night, there are three women missing.' They went out for a smoke, which they were given by those horrible people, and never came back. We were ordered to get out of the house as quickly as possible. No one knew what was going on. As we all stood there in front of the house, they started giving us instructions where to go. No one knew where we were going to or what to look forward to. Exhausted, famished, dehydrated . . . we headed through the biggest war zone on that side of Bosnia. It was 30°C and we were without food or water. The closest village was twenty kilometres away. There were old women dying on their feet. We couldn't do anything about it then, just leave them on the side of the street and save ourselves. I walked with my mum, brother and some other relatives through the emptiness of the village, city, world, whatever you want to call it. I'd never seen such things before. Even my mum said she never saw such an inhumanity in this world, even in the movies. There were dead bodies lying everywhere and some even hanging down the fences. But the thing that caught my eye wasn't the people who had died because I'd seen my grandmother dead: it was the people who were slaughtered and the babies that a dumb person could tell were killed with bare hands.

My father was taken away before this experience. Now our thoughts focused on his destiny. We knew that he was taken to a different camp with the rest of the men from the town we stayed at, but if he was alive no one knew. We heard that there were a few camps set up, but that from one of them, no man came out alive. All we could hope for was that he wasn't taken to a death camp. Every day we asked ourselves if he was suffering from pain. Or did he manage to escape from wherever they took him? Maybe he was back at home but that wasn't safe either.

I didn't know that it would take six months to see him again, nor did I know that my new home would be Australia.

Journey to Freedom

by Hai-Van Nguyen, aged 18

155980, 155981: My parents hold the numbers, scrawled hurriedly in the impermanence of chalk, across their chests. The camera flashes come in methodical succession, and in a brief moment they become mere faces attached to numbers. There had been many before them and there would be many after them. Away from the sharp focus of the lens, my parents blur into insignificance – indistinguishable faces in a crowd that is a common statistic.

My parents recite the numbers precisely to me as we sit around the kitchen bench. My mother sits across from me, having not had time to remove the apron from her chest. My father has just arrived home from work, the front of his shirt drenched in the fumes of assorted chemicals. They've come a long way from having had a number held across their chests and it amazes me they recall them so easily. 'It's something one never forgets,' my mother says. 'You wear it in your mind,' she says, 'long after the chalk has been erased.' A prisoner never forgets his number.

Society is obsessed with numbers. Long after the human atrocities have occurred, all we remember are the numbers. We remember there were six million victims of the Holocaust and one million casualties during the Vietnam War. More recently, we hear about the '765 people' who are 'unauthorised boat arrivals' and the '228 detainees'; currently in 'detention' in Woomera.

We're hearing politicians justify their actions with phrases like 'Australia is accepting an ample number of refugees for an industrialised country.' As usual issues involving human lives become overshadowed by numbers that relegate people to the status of mere statistics. We remember the numbers, but we forget the human faces behind them. We forget that people, whether they be refugees or not, are mothers, fathers, wives, husbands, sons and daughters.

History books and newspapers purport to telling the facts, but facts do not only consist of numbers. Human experience is real; human suffering is real, and so are the stories that capture them. We need stories to restore the human face to such atrocities. Stories, in capturing the triumphs and sorrows of each individual's experience, will serve a wider purpose of giving a collective voice to all humanity. They capture humanity's innate sense of endurance and the human spirit's capacity to survive. Numbers become concrete and meaningless. Stories, in essence, are timeless, transcendent. We need these stories to give human faces, not numbers, to the refugees who arrive on our shores; to refugees used as numbers in an unbalanced political and social equation. This is one of those stories.

My parents have been in Australia for almost fourteen years, but scarcely does the number come up. They measure the years not by days, but by the experiences that have accumulated during their long 'Hanh Trinh Tim Tu Do'* – the tears, the laughter, the backbreaking work and the triumphs. Throughout my childhood, I have heard fragments of our experience fleeing Vietnam, like snippets of an old, barely visible movie. My memories are few and far between, but my parents recall it with vivid accuracy. On that Thursday evening, they told their story for the first time.

My father said the trip had been planned for months. The vessel that would take us to our freedom was a dishevelled,

*Amongst Vietnamese people, these are the words many refugees use to describe their experience. It means 'journey to freedom'.

barely sea-worthy fishing boat about twelve metres long and three metres wide. It could only hold about forty people, but would be forced to hold twice its capacity. The night we left my mother recalls having never said goodbye to my grandparents – she could not even tell them we were going. It was a heart-breaking deception, but much like what we experienced as refugees, it was done out of necessity, not choice. Before we left, the boat was loaded with cargo, in the hopes that it would hide the human cargo it was to contain. At that time, many were still fleeing Vietnam and the authorities fiercely guarded the coasts. Only several years earlier, if you were caught trying to escape you would have been shot. At the time we chose to leave, if you were caught, you were captured and imprisoned.

We left just after the last drops of light had trickled from the horizon. The final glimpse any of us got of our homeland was of a large black mass of land and the distinct silhouette of wind-ruffled coconut palms. I was four, my sister was eight and my bother was ten. My parents shielded me from the pain of the experience through deception, much in the same way they had my grandparents. Each time I asked, 'where are we going', my mother would assure me we were simply 'going to Saigon'. Her words did not subdue my childish sense of curiosity – every few hours I would ask 'why is it taking so long?' and every time she would reply 'it only seems long'.

The next morning we were out of Vietnamese waters and well on our way across the South China Sea. We had overcome the first obstacle, but any security we felt was brief because we knew of the potential dangers that lay ahead. The greatest fear confronting all Vietnamese refugee boats at that time was having to cross the waters of Thailand and come across a Thai fishing boat. These boats were occupied by people whose brutal acts had earned them the title of pirates. They deliberately sought out Vietnamese fishing boats, knowing we were vulnerable. They were most interested in our belongings, but that was not all they stole. Girls were kidnapped, raped and eventually sold into slavery or prostitution. Approaching the waters of Thailand, we knew many of the stories we'd heard could easily become a reality. It was the sight of a boat in the distance that made my father choke with fear. He urged the captain to connect the spare motor and make the boat go faster. Below deck fear spread quicker than the lice that infested our bodies. The women shrivelled up, fearing that their short, cropped hair and masculine clothes would not be enough to pass them off as men. Eventually our boat sped away from them, but had we been an inch too slow, many of us would probably not have been here today.

The boat, with its human cargo of eighty, was stuffy and unstable. On numerous occasions, giant waves hurled over the sides and splashed onto the decks – we were almost certain the boat would capsize. Three days into our voyage we came across a large cargo ship. We screamed from below deck, with what little energy we had, hoping they would take us aboard. They never did.

All we had to eat were these strange cakes made of dried rice coated with sugar. Oranges were a luxury.

The odour was unbearable – the smell of urine and vomit mingled with the smell of fear. At times you would wake up the next morning to find someone else's vomit in your hair. It was hard, but we had to keep reminding ourselves that we were all in the same boat, literally and metaphorically. Bodies were entangled, overlapping so you no longer knew where somebody else's arm started and yours ended. For the brief time that some of us got to go on deck, all that met our gaze was a hollow sky and an empty sea. We were but a tiny speck of life wedged between a sandwich of two equally brutal and unforgiving forces. The sea that encircled us promised everything and nothing at the same time. Our freedom was the deadly kind.

After five days and four nights we finally reached Malaysia. At that point, anything, even a refugee camp, was better than the unstable confines of the ocean. Of the boats that headed towards this very place, most never made it. To say that we were lucky is an understatement. We were put onto a desert island called Bidong and placed in an area enclosed by barbwires. The camp was a virtual prison, so for months we were forced to serve a prison term, not knowing what offence it was we had committed. We, like many others, found ourselves living by a tight routine – work by day and sleep by night – not knowing that the word refugee had take on the same meaning as the word criminal. Food and water were strictly rationed. All we were given to eat was rice and each person was given only a gallon of water each day for drinking and washing. There was never enough to go around, and if you missed out, well then . . . you missed out.

The water flows abundantly as my mother stands there washing up the dishes. My father sits across from me, cleaning up the last grains of rice on his bowl until there is nothing left. As soon as he is done, he lifts up his shift to show me the scars that are still faintly but permanently carved into his back. 'I got these while trying to steal some water,' he says, almost laughing. One time some of us missed out on water rations so he and my uncle attempted to steal some from the supplies reserved for the following day's handout. When they were caught, they were beaten by Malaysian guards.

During the day, my parents did farm work. They harvested crops, planted and raked the soil. They, like so many others, struggled to grasp the irony that they had come all that way only to relive the very lives they had been trying to escape. There were some who were forced to pass the time by fishing instead. Most never returned from their week-long, sometimes month-long trips, and so were inevitably lost to the same sea they thought they had overcome.

Six aching months passed, and still there was no word as to what would happen to us, but uncertainty was nothing new. It could be years before we were accepted. Or worse, we could be denied acceptance and simply be shipped back to where we had come from. Finally, our number was called. MC249. It was the number of our boat. My parents remember that number too. Finally, we were no longer nobody, we had become a number. The joy of finally being accepted however, was overshadowed by the grief of those who were left behind, and even worse, of those who were forced to go back.

The running water drowns out my mother's tears, but I can see her wipe her eyes as she tells me of the haunting images still vividly emblazoned in her mind. 'Some prayed at the feet of authorities. Some set themselves alight. Others cut their stomachs open in protest. Thousands fainted as they were dragged back onto ships to be transported home. There was a family who lived in the cabin next to ours – two parents and two children. They committed suicide when they were told they could not go forward. That was the worst.'

We arrived in Australia on 23rd October 1989. We had lived to tell a story some never could. But the battle was not over, in fact, it was just beginning. We had fought with the elements and with authorities, but the real battle started the day we arrived in Australia. My parents have since learnt that language barriers can be as insurmountable as giant waves, that exclusions leave a void far greater than the size of any ocean and that numbers last long after they have been removed. There is, however, another face to the tribulations they have been forced to endure: there is nothing that brings out genuine human endeavour and courage more than the refugee experience. There's nothing like having to cling to every bare breath, to see life reduced to a scarce trickle, to walk the tightrope separating life and death, at times not knowing one from the other. Very rarely do we get to see human nature stripped of all that it depends on to learn that human nature is itself enough.

The radio blaring frantically in the background now turns its attention to the 'refugee crisis'. Once again, it is the numbers we hear first. '. . . fifty detainees have escaped from a detention centre in . . .' Fourteen years on, my parents still remember their numbers (and I am sure they always will) but it no longer defines who they are. Having told their story, they have embedded themselves in history, and if not official history, then certainly personal history. They are no longer part of a statistic, but a personal legacy that I will pass onto my children. The refugees that have recently arrived on the shores of Australia still continue to be numbers, to be statistics, to be overlooked. Children whose faces we see peering out from behind the wire lattice of our detention centres are still one of 'fifty detained children' and their parents continue to be one of '65 females' or '105 males.' Perhaps, as a society, we should focus less on numbers and more on words – words of compassion, words of kindness and words of human value. Most importantly, we should listen to their words, hear their voices and document their stories.

Acknowledgements

These essays and stories were encouraged, collected, selected, admired, promoted, collated and edited with the help of a huge number of people and organisations, including: Actors For Refugees; Phillip Adams; A Just Australia/Australians For Just Refugee Programs; Allen & Unwin; Amnesty International Australia; Ian Anderson; Australian Education Union; Australian Education Union – South Australia; Australian Refugees Association; Kate Atkinson; BJ and A Baker; Andrew Bentley; Geraldine Brooks; Julian Burnside; Errin Davis; Sue Cass; James Dent; Jenni Devereaux; Kate Durham; Dan Farmer; Ann Feather; Derek Fielding; Malcolm Fraser; Ron and Sue Fraser; Mary Freer; Fremantle Refugee Support Project; Raimond Gaita; Alice Garner; Helen Garner; Charlotte George; Libby Gleeson; Virginia Gordon; Mariana Hardwick; Lolo Houbein; Annette Hughes; Independent Education Union Australia; John Kinsella; Katie Langmore; Jeremy Lindsay-Taylor; Kevin Liston; Sam Malin; The CUB Malthouse; Kelly Martin; Tom Mann; Meme McDonald; Bern McPhee; Joan Medhurst; Metro/Screen Education; Neil Montieth; Gaylene Morgan; National Committee on Human Rights Education; NSW Teachers Federation; Oz Positive; CJR and LJ Payne; Project Safecom; Hellen Rabel; Lea Redfern; Resources for Courses; Margaret Reynolds United Nations Association Australia; Margaret Riches; Rural Australians for

Refugees; Roger Sallis; Savoy Park Plaza Hotel; School of Social Work and Social Policy, University of South Australia; Selina; Simone Senisin; Tom Shapcott; Albert Shelling; Beverley Sherry; Jack Smit; MDH and REJ Smith; South Australians for Justice for Refugees; Jo Stanley; Helena Turinski; Victoria Chambers; Victorian Trades Hall Council; Franziska Wagenfeld; Nadia Wheatley; Amanda Whitmore; Morag White; John Wishart; Diana Wolowski; Ulrike Zimmermann.

Many more unnamed teachers and parents across Australia made this book possible. They inspired and helped their children and young adults to take up the project and produce these stories. Most of all this book owes its existence to the children and young adults who wrote essays and stories for the competition. There were many wonderful pieces that do not appear here, simply for lack of space.

Lucy McBride's essay was published in *Screen Education* February 2003. Hai-Van Nguyen's essay was published in *Newsmonth* December 2002; *Education* February 2003; *Fairfield Champions*; *Physical Journeys: The Complete Guide to the HSC Area of Study: The Journey* 2003; *AIR! Winning Stories* 2002; and, abridged, in *The Age* December 4th 2002. Melanie Poole's essay was read on Radio National in Lea Redfern's Radio Eye documentary 'A Place You Cannot Imagine' 29th March 2003; and published in *AIR! Winning Stories* 2002. Zara al-Hosany al-Shara's story was published in *Educator* March 2003 and in *AIR! Winning Stories* 2002. Alexandra Drakulic's story was published in *Stories From a Troubled Homeland* and *Roads to Refuge*. Essays and stories of Khazmira Bashah, Rosa Brown, Gabriel Courtney, Zana Mujezinovic, Tita Tran and Mohammad Zia were published in *AIR! Winning Stories* 2002.

About the Contributors Now

Pharan Akhtarkhavari

Pharan was born in Sydney on the 11th of February into a Persian Baha'i family. He understands what the Baha'is in Iran went through during the Islamic Revolution. Pharan feels that the story of his uncle sums up what happened to the majority of Persian Baha'is during that dreadful period in Iran. He is now living in Brisbane with his family feeling content with his life and living life to the max! He is proud to be Australian.

Yasmin Aleem

I am currently in my first year at Flinders University, South Australia, studying a Bachelor of Behavioural Science. I hope to do Honours and Masters and Psychology and my dream job is to work in a refugee camp overseas.

Ghulam-e-Ali

Lives in Victoria.

Mohammad Riyadh Ali

Mohammad arrived recently from Iraq with his family to settle permanently in Australia. He lives in Victoria.

Zara Al-Hosany Al-Shara
I am a year ten student in NSW. I like public speaking and debating and enjoy horse riding. My favourite subjects are English and Commerce. In the future I'd love to be lawyer.

Khazmira Bashah
Khazmira Bashah – Human rights activist! Ambition: Heart Surgeon or Politician. Goals: To make the world a more tolerant place. To establish a program to ensure that children (especially girls) in Third World Countries have access to books and are taught to read.

Adam Bennett
I am currently studying year nine. My favourite subjects are computer programming and business studies. I enjoy playing golf – I am of a twenty-six handicap and I have recently moved to southern Queensland from South Australia.

Bojana Bokan
Lives in Queensland.

Rosa Brown
I am in year eight. I like to row and read books about the world and social issues. I care about human rights and equality.

Sarah-Jane Bryson
I was born in Wagga Wagga, NSW, to a large family. Shortly afterwards we moved to a quiet suburb in Queensland where we still live today. My interests include reading, music and the arts. I will continue my studies after school in the areas of journalism and business.

Chloe Costas
Chloe completed year twelve in 2002 and has been spending 2003 working and travelling around Europe. In 2004 she will commence a Bachelor of International Studies at the University of New South Wales.

Gabriel Courtney

I live with my mum in Sydney and my dad lives in London. I went to India for eighteen months from 1999 to 2000 with my mum for her research. I went to school there and learnt to speak Hindi and play *tabla*, a kind of double drum. All my friends there were very poor, but good at lots of things like kite flying. I am in year six. I like reading novels, playing computer and I go to drama at the Australian Theatre for Young People (ATYP) at the Wharf theatre.

Nitya Dambiec

What should I tell you about myself that is important? I would like in my life to do something useful for others because every person is a part of my family and I have this responsibility. Also, I am an optimist and the future is bright because the only lasting achievements are those carried out by the people who really care.

Zac Darab

My name is Zachi Darab and I am currently in senior studies at high school in New South Wales. When I leave school I plan to travel the world and study medicine at University.

Gracia Diep

I am currently in year eleven. My interests include spending time with my friends and cooking. My goal is to gain entrance to a degree in business at university. My motto in life is never give up because you never know what can happen.

Alexandra Drakulic

At the moment I am studying accounting but have applied for the NSW Police Force. Next July I plan to go to Vietnam to visit my World Vision sponsor child.

Aidan Fawkes

I'm currently sixteen and studying as a high school student. I love soccer, camping and music, especially rock and punk. After school I'm hoping to go to university and end up involved with event management or in the media industry.

Rosie Giudici

I'm fourteen and my name is Rosie. I live in Tasmania and I have two brothers. I love holidays and my favourite subject at school is art. I really can't wait to travel and I love to have fun!

Mina Hami

I'm seventeen years old and in year twelve. I arrived in Australia in 1998 with my family. My plans are to continue my education through university studying Arts in Communication and Humanities.

Helen Huynh

I like to question things, anything, whether or not it has an answer. Perhaps it was this curiosity that led me to ask Kim his story. What I did here was put a question mark next to my perception of things, challenging the reality I took for granted as the only one.

Tshala Jenkins

Lives in NSW.

Chelsea June

I am interested in reading, dancing and music. I am in year eight so don't do much studying but I love school. My plans for the future are to finish school up to year twelve, then go to uni and become a lawyer either in criminal law or family law.

Jack Lander

I like sport and at the moment I am playing indoor hockey. I also play grass hockey, soccer and baseball. My three favourite subjects at school are cooking, Italian and woodwork. My future goal in life is either to become a pro ice hockey player or grass hockey player. I have four sisters, Megan, Heather, Stacey and Rochelle and my two parents, Dave and Julie.

Lucy McBride

Lucy spent 2003 – having completed year twelve last year – working in Adelaide. Now Lucy has gone to Botswana for four months working as a teacher's aide. Next year she hopes to study either medicine or veterinary science.

Hannah Moore

Hannah is currently a year twelve student. She has been very involved with the recent refugees but hopes to study acting. Hannah aims to advocate for refugees in both her writing and her visual art work.

Karen Motta

Lives in Western Australia.

Zana Mujezinovic

Lives in Victoria.

Hai-Van Nguyen

I'm nineteen years old. I was born in Vietnam. I have an older brother and sister. My main interests including poetry, literature, writing and travelling. My favourite poets are Sylvia Plath and Robert Gray and my favourite authors Anais Nin and Michael Ondaatje. I'd love to travel to Africa and South America and do further exploration of my home country of Vietnam. I'm currently studying Law/International Studies at the University of New South Wales. I would love to get into the areas of human rights law and immigration law. One day I'd love to work for the United Nations. My goals are to help refugees, earn enough money to buy my parents a big house and to one day hopefully write a novel.

Katie Petrie

Lives in Queensland.

Simon Pitt

Simon Pitt is a Tasmanian student with a passion for youth and international affairs. He enjoys contributing to his community, and is active in roles both at school and extramurally. Simon is a keen debater and public speaker, and especially enjoys the way in which these endeavors challenge people to consider their own viewpoints from different perspectives, and rationalise their positions.

Melanie Poole

Melanie Poole is an energetic person who enjoys writing, public speaking and travel and has successfully pursued these interests while studying. Melanie has always worked to support global justice and human rights. She feels particularly strongly about the Australian Government's treatment of asylum seekers, and is interested in international law. Melanie is studying law at ANU.

Zina Romanov

I was born in the USSR. Arrived in Australia in 1993. I have always had a passion for writing and people. I am a student in UNSW (BA Social Science-Economics). My career plans are to be a financial analyst and eventually move into politics, writing in retirement. I am planning to go on a world tour in a year or so before finishing my degree. I also love France and would love to live there one day. I am currently learning French.

Ariel Smith

I am the youngest member of the Australian Greens. In the future my long term goal is to get a degree in Law and also a degree in Environmental Engineering. On the 30th of September I turn fourteen. The Tampa calamity changed my life forever and opened my mind to the people and their plights through-out troubled parts of the world.

Tita Tran

I was born in Vietnam. My dad (a heart doctor) is dead and my mum used to be an anaesthetist. We flew over to Australia, where I went to different schools. I now live with my mum and sister. I'm currently in high school and hope to stay all five years and get a good job in the medical area.

Nooria Wazefadost

I would like to be a doctor in my future. My interest is to help others in their difficulties. I also like one day to see every one treated equally. Human beings are human beings. There is no such difference.

Jane Woodward

Jane is a seventeen-year-old student in year twelve in Canberra. She works part time as a swimming instructor and is an enthusiastic rower and triathlete. She also enjoys reading and writing.

Mohammad Zia

Mohammad is originally from Afghanistan. He arrived in Australia just over three years ago and still has no certainty about his future. He finished high school in 2002. Mohammad is now studying first year Computer Science at Victoria University.

Jumping to Heaven

Stories about refugee children

Katherine Goode for the Children's Interests Bureau

Neary plunged her hand into the bag and pulled out two long elastic chains. 'It a Cambodian game,' she said. 'It's called Jumping to the Heavens. *You must jump very high. But don't worry. If you have trouble, I'll jump and save you.'*

The stories in *Jumping to Heaven* are based on the true experiences of refugee children who have migrated to Australia. Their stories are sad, scary, thought-provoking and sometimes funny. Above all they are stories of courage and hope, sometimes against overwhelming odds.

For more information visit www.wakefieldpress.com.au

Desert Sorrow

Asylum seekers at Woomera

Tom Mann

'*Desert Sorrow* gives an extraordinary and important insight into the secret daily life behind the wire of detention centres.

'The unassuming but potent book is a must read, an eye witness testament to a phase in Australia's history that has been deliberately hidden and is still destroying the lives of men women and children.'

Eva Sallis

For more information visit www.wakefieldpress.com.au